DOCTOR WHO
ARC OF INFINITY

DOCTOR WHO
ARC OF INFINITY

Based on the BBC television serial by Johnny Byrne by
arrangement with the British Broadcasting Corporation

Terrance Dicks

No. 80 in the Doctor Who Library

A TARGET BOOK
Published by
the Paperback Division of
W. H. ALLEN & Co. Ltd

A Target Book
Published in 1983
by the Paperback Division of W. H. Allen & Co. Ltd.
A Howard & Wyndham Company
44 Hill Street, London W1X 8LB

First published in Great Britain by
W. H. Allen & Co. Ltd 1983
Reprinted 1984

Printed and bound in Great Britain by
Anchor Brendon Ltd, Tiptree, Essex

ISBN 0 426 19342 3

Contents

DOCTOR WHO
ARC OF INFINITY

1

Deadly Meeting

They met in a hidden chamber, deep beneath the Capitol: the being from another dimension, and the Time Lord who was betraying not only his people but his Universe.

The Time Lord slipped a cube-shaped code key into a complex control-device. There was an upward-rushing fountain of green light, and a projection of the alien appeared. The tall, cloaked figure wore an elaborately stylised mask. There was an ornate medallion on its chest, and the figure appeared negative rather than positive, since it was not in its proper Universe.

The Time Lord sat in darkness beyond the circle of light.

'You have made your choice?' demanded the alien.

'Yes. We are ready to begin.'

'Excellent! And who is it to be?'

'It has not been easy. Because of time, present location, personality – for these and other reasons, it must be the Doctor.'

For a moment the alien seemed startled. 'The Doctor?' Then he chuckled eerily. 'Yes, most ingenious. A perfect, choice, Time Lord.'

The light dimmed and the alien faded away.

The Time Lord rose and went to begin his betrayal.

In the Capitol computer room everything was peaceful. But then, it always was. Two brown-robed specialist computer technicians were going about their duties, surrounded by the humming banks of equipment. The older of the two, a thin, balding Gallifreyan, was called Talor. The other was a good-looking young technican named Damon.

Suddenly a warning light began blinking on the main console. Damon went over to investigate, while Talor looked on intrigued. Emergencies were rare here.

'It's the security circuit,' said Damon, puzzled. 'Cut the scrambler, will you?'

Talor operated a control and the warning light cut out. Damon lifted an access flap, extracted a circuit and studied it thoughtfully. 'That's odd. There's a photon cell burn-out.'

He took a replacement circuit from a nearby rack and slipped it in place. 'I'd better check the data bank's unharmed.' He touched another control and reacted in surprise as a screen lit up. It was filled with a steadily unrolling blur of complex symbols. 'I don't believe it. Someone's transmitting bio-data!'

Talor came to join him. 'What is it?'

Damon stared disbelievingly at the screen. 'It's the bio-data extract of one of the Time Lords!'

Talon was horrified. 'Cut it! Cut it at once!'

Damon obeyed and the screen went dark.

'This is treason,' said Talor worriedly. 'I must report it immediately.'

He hurried from the computer room.

Sometimes even a Time Lord never seems to have quite

2

enough time. Little jobs pile up, things get in the way . . .

The Doctor was tackling one such little job now, feeling the sense of virtuous efficiency that comes when you finally catch up on some task that should have been done ages ago.

He was in one of the TARDIS corridors, working at the jumble of equipment behind a roundel that had been removed from the wall. Now in his fifth incarnation, the Doctor was a slightly-built, fair-haired young man in the dress of an Edwardian cricketer – striped trousers, fawn frock-coat with red piping, white sweater and open-necked shirt.

Watching him was a brown-haired girl with fine, rather aristocratic features. She wore a kind of velvet trouser-suit with elaborately puffed sleeves. This was his current companion, Nyssa of Traken. The product of a highly technological society, and a bio-electronics expert in her own right, Nyssa felt that the Doctor ran the TARDIS in far too haphazard a manner.

The Doctor made a final adjustment to the audio-circuit, and slotted it back in place. 'Such a simple little repair job really!'

'Quite,' said Nyssa pointedly. 'Why didn't you do it sooner?'

'Well, you know how it is,' said the Doctor vaguely. 'You put things off for a day. Next thing you know it's a hundred years later and it's still not done.'

Nyssa sighed, realising she was never going to get the Doctor properly organised. 'Never mind, it's done now. It'll be nice to have audio link-up on the scanner again.'

The Doctor replaced the roundel. 'Let's go and see if it works!'

Robin Stuart stood on one of Amsterdam's innumerable picturesque bridges, staring gloomily down at the waters of the canal. The colourful bustling street-scene was all around him, but Robin was too worried to take it in.

Wearing jeans and anorak, loaded down with a great bulging pack like a turtle carrying his own home, Robin Stuart looked exactly like all the other young people who spend their summers wandering around Europe. There aren't quite so many of them these days. Some of the big capital cities have become cold and unwelcoming. But not friendly old Amsterdam. The Dutch are a tolerant people, willing to turn a blind eye to such crimes as being young and hard-up.

Robin turned and walked along the bridge to the telephone kiosk at the far end. Another back-pack, fully as big as his own, was propped up outside, and inside was another very similar young man. His friend Colin Frazer was currently engaged in an endless telephone conversation with some mysterious cousin or other, who was due to come out to Amsterdam to visit them the following day.

The door of the box was propped open and Robin could hear Colin's familiar Australian twang. 'No, everywhere's full, we've got to sleep rough tonight. We'll be at the hostel from tomorrow, though – that's the number I gave you.' He nodded to Robin, and said, 'Look, I've got to go now. I'll see you at the airport tomorrow. Take care.'

He came out of the kiosk. Robin helped him on with his pack and said, 'Everything okay?'

'Yes, she'll be – what's the matter?'

Robin had suddenly tensed and turned away, and was staring at the canal with apparent fascination. 'Oh no! A policeman,' he whispered.

A large Dutch policeman was strolling along on the other side of the road. It was quite obvious to Colin that the policeman was enjoying the pleasant spring day, and wasn't the slightest bit interested in them. But all the same Robin was quite unable to relax until the policeman had gone by.

Colin grinned. 'It's all right, Robin. The Dutch are a civilised race. They don't put people in prison for losing a passport.'

'No, but they do deport you, though!'

A couple of nights ago, Robin's passport had been stolen in one of Amsterdam's crowded cafés, though luckily the thief had missed his wallet. Colin had suggested Robin report the loss of the passport to the police, the British Embassy, or both, but Robin didn't want to – not yet. He was convinced that reporting the loss would mean an official telling-off, hundreds of forms to fill in, and, worst of all, the immediate ending of his holiday, since he'd be packed off home at once. He knew he'd have to report the loss sooner or later, but he was determined to put it off till the last possible moment.

Unfortunately, Robin was a bit of a worrier by nature. The loss of his passport made him feel like a stateless person, and he went round acting like the proverbial man-on-the-run every time he saw a policeman.

'It's all right,' said Colin. 'He's gone. Let's go and get something to eat. Then we've got to find a place to sleep tonight.'

Robin said, 'I was going to tell you, I think I found somewhere when I was wandering around earlier. I did a bit of exploring. Not the most appealing place in the

5

world, but central – and very cheap.'

'Sounds perfect. Not too noisy, is it?'

Robin smiled. 'Quiet as the grave!'

'Perfect!' said the Doctor.

They were in the TARDIS control room checking on the scanner's newly installed audio facility. The scanner screen was switched on. At the moment it showed nothing but the black emptiness of deep space.

Nyssa smiled. 'So now we've got an audio system, but nothing to listen to!'

The Doctor switched off the scanner. 'And nothing to look at either. Couldn't be better. Peace and quiet, just what the Doctor ordered.'

He was halfway to the door when Nyssa said sternly, 'Doctor!'

'What?'

'There are lots of other repairs that need doing, you know.'

'Really,' said the Doctor guiltily. 'There's nothing urgent, is there?'

'There's the navigational system,' said Nyssa. 'There must be something wrong with it. We never seem to arrive where we intend to!'

'Ah well,' said the Doctor apologetically. 'Ever since those Cybermen damaged the console – '

'And there's another thing,' Nyssa went on. 'Didn't you say the control room was in a state of temporal grace – guns couldn't be fired there?'

'Ah well,' said the Doctor again. 'No one's perfect, you know.'

And before Nyssa could say any more he slipped out of the door.

Suddenly a light started blinking on the console.

Nyssa studied it for a moment and then called, 'Doctor!'

Strolling along the corridor, the Doctor heard Nyssa's voice, but decided to pretend he hadn't. She called again. 'Doctor, please! Come quickly.'

Catching the note of panic in her voice, the Doctor turned and hurried back to the control room.

Once again the Time Lord and his alien confederate were in conference, the Time Lord in his chair, the alien enclosed in the cone of light.

'The data has been received, Time Lord,' said the alien. 'But not the booster element. Why?'

'I had to close down transmission. A fault developed.'

'What will you do now?'

'Check to see if my transmission of the bio-data was detected.'

'And if it was?'

'Then I will deal with the matter. Perhaps we should delay until I am certain.'

'It is too late,' said the alien coldly. 'The TARDIS is already under my control.'

The Doctor stood brooding over the console. It was easy to see why Nyssa had called him back. 'According to the sensors we're converging with a massive source of magnetic radiation.'

Nyssa had switched on the scanner and was studying the screen. 'But there's nothing out there. Just light-years of black, empty space.'

'Well, something's causing these readings,' said the Doctor thoughtfully. 'We'd better change course.'

'Where to?'

'"Anywhere! Just so long as it's away from here.'

The Doctor began working furiously at the controls.

Robin led Colin through the busy streets of central
Amsterdam, into a quiet back street, and finally to a
beautiful old-fashioned house, set back off the road in
its own grounds.

Colin looked at it, a little overwhelmed. 'We're
spending the night in there?'

Robin grinned. 'Well – in a way!'

Suddenly the TARDIS control room started to judder.

'What's happening?' asked Nyssa.

The Doctor was frantically busy at the controls. 'I
don't know!'

Nyssa studied the console. 'These readings Doctor –
they just don't make any sense!'

'I know,' said the Doctor and went on with his work.

Robin led Colin through the beautifully kept, formal
gardens to a point some little way from the house. Colin
looked around nervously, expecting to be nabbed as a
trespasser any minute, but the whole place seemed
deserted.

They stopped at an old stone fountain with water
spouting from bowls held by reclining figures. Beside it
stood an iron grille, which led to a flight of stone steps
leading downwards.

Robin made for the steps and started to descend.

'Hey, where are you going?' called Colin.

'Just follow me.'

Somewhat dubiously, Colin followed.

The steps led down into darkness, and Colin found it
all rather eerie. 'What is this place? Why is it so dark?'

Robin fished out a torch and handed it over. 'Here,

try this. Trust me, Colin. Have I ever led you astray?'

Colin flashed the torch to light the way ahead. 'There's always a first time. Who owns this place anyway?'

'The State, I imagine. It's a kind of forgotten national treasure. No one ever comes here – except the odd gardener during the day.'

There was an arched doorway at the bottom of the steps. Robin went through it and Colin followed, flashing the torch around. They were in a kind of cellar – a cavernous place lined with carved stone tombs. Some of the tombs had effigies sculpted on them.

All around there were stone columns, carved angels, death masks on the walls – the whole effect was very creepy indeed.

'Hey, wait a minute. This is a crypt,' said Colin indignantly.

'Didn't you realise?' asked Robin in mock surprise. 'You saw the ornamentation outside, the fountain . . .'

'I thought it was just some kind of cellar. Are you serious – about spending the night here?'

'Of course.'

Colin shone his torch around the crypt. Cold stone faces leered back at him. Somewhere there was the curiously sinister sound of dripping water. 'Now I know you're crazy!'

'Well, not exactly in here,' said Robin. 'Come on, our little nest's through here.' He led the way to a door at the far end of the crypt, unbolted it and led the way through.

The cellar on the other side of the door was considerably more reassuring. It was smaller and more modern, and the air felt warm and dry. A complex apparatus of giant pipes and dials and turn-cocks lined the walls. Colin saw another door at the far end. 'What is this place?'

'A pumping house. Not exactly the Ritz, but it's dry and warm.'

Colin could hear a steady humming coming from the tangle of machinery. 'What's in the pipes?'

'Water. We're below sea-level here. Stop the pumps, and Amsterdam would have to take up its stilts and float.' Robin looked round with an air of proprietary pride. 'Well, how do you like it?'

'All right, I suppose,' said Colin grudgingly. 'I'm not too keen on the neighbours though.'

Sticking the torch on a convenient ledge, Robin shrugged out of his pack and started to unpack his sleeping-bag. Colin could see his friend was proud of the place he'd found, and in a way you couldn't blame him. There was a lot to be said for it. Clean and dry, quiet, completely private, and best of all completely free. But all the same – a crypt!

Colin had seen horror movies about young people spending the night in graveyards and haunted houses.

Something always happened to them – something *frightful*.

Telling himself he was being silly, Colin got on with his preparations for the night – unaware that this particular crypt held terrors beyond his worst imaginings.

2

The Horror in the Crypt

Damon looked up from his instrument-check as Talor came into the computer room. 'The analysis checks out. It was the Doctor's bio-data extract that was being transmitted. What did the Castellan have to say?'

'Nothing, as yet. Despite the urgency of my request, he chooses not to be available until tomorrow.'

'You realise only a member of the High Council could have been transmitting that data?'

'I do,' said Talor grimly. 'We'll just have to wait until tomorrow.'

Damon stood up. 'Very well. Do you need me any more?'

'No. Goodnight.'

'Goodnight,' said Damon. Picking up a data file he made his way out of the computer room, passing through the quietly humming rows of data banks and disappearing through the door at the far end.

Talor sat lost in thought, unaware that the door behind him, the door through which he himself had entered, was opening slowly.

He heard movement, turned, and saw that he had a distinguished visitor. 'Good evening, my Lord.'

The visitor made no reply, but produced a hand-blaster, a bulbous affair with a transparent barrel.

11

Talor stared at it in disbelief. 'An impulse laser?'

He still couldn't quite realise what was happening to him – not until a blast of light shot from the barrel, blasting him down. Talor seemed to shrivel up and his body slumped to the floor.

The Time Lord went over to the console at which Damon had been working, lifted a flap, and worked briefly on the complex circuitry beneath. He raised his weapon and fired, sending sparks shooting from the console. Then he stepped over Talor's body and left the computer room.

With a last worried look round the pumping chamber, Colin prepared to climb into his sleeping-bag.

Robin, who was already comfortably snuggled down by now, watched him with some amusement. 'Are you really going to sleep like that?'

'Like what?'

'Fully dressed. You've even got your boots on!'

'I'm not taking any chances,' said Colin stubbornly.

'Oh come on. It's only a pump house. The worse that can happen is that we get caught by some kind of caretaker and turfed out.'

'It's just that I find this place – spooky.'

'You could at least risk taking your boots off!'

'I suppose so.' Sitting on his sleeping-bag, Colin began unlacing his boots.

The renegade Time Lord said, 'It is as I feared. The transmission was detected. But the matter has been dealt with.'

The alien shimmered eerily in his cone of light. 'How?'

The Time Lord smiled. 'The one who detected and

12

reported the transmission has been disposed of.'

'Then bonding can take place immediately?'

There was a pause and then the Time Lord said reluctantly, 'You are sure there is no other way?'

'I am not of your dimensions, Time Lord. I have the means to enter, but without the physical imprint of bonding, I cannot remain among you.'

The Doctor wrestled frantically with the controls, but it was no good. 'I can't control the TARDIS!'

'Can't you over-ride the controls?'

'I've just tried that. It's hopeless.'

Nyssa was staring at the scanner screen. 'Doctor, look!'

A ball of light was arcing towards them across the blackness of space.

The Doctor stared at it in fascination. 'Something's breaking through! Is it a materialisation?' asked Nyssa.

'I'm not sure. Something from another dimension, I think.'

The ball of light flared brighter, rushing towards the TARDIS at incredible speed. Around it, space seemed to boil and churn, as if the very fabric of the Universe was being disturbed.

'Quick, Nyssa, let's get out of here!' shouted the Doctor.

They ran from the control room, and as they ran the entire room seemed to twist and distort. A blur of light burst through the scanner screen into the control room, and the ball of fire poured all its energies into the TARDIS. Suddenly an up-rushing fountain of green light appeared in the control room.

The Doctor and Nyssa ran down the corridor, and there too the walls seemed to twist and bend about

13

them. Their movements slowed and they had an eerie sensation of running without making progress.

In the control room, the flaring energy resolved itself into a cone of light embodying a strange alien being, and then it moved off in pursuit of the Doctor.

As the Doctor and Nyssa struggled vainly to make some progress along the corridor, the weirdly distorted form of the alien sped towards them.

The Doctor watched helplessly as the apparition bore down on him. It reached him – and enveloped him.

Nyssa watched in horror as the alien shape absorbed the Doctor for a moment, then suddenly faded.

The Doctor stood rigid, his face twisted in agony, and then slid to the ground.

It was the frantic gurgling of the pipes that woke Colin. The noise grew louder and louder, rising to a kind of frenzy. There was something else mingled with it, a strange wheezing, groaning sound. Eventually the rising crescendo of sound penetrated Colin's uneasy sleep and he awoke, eyes wide open in fright. Light was pulsing beneath the door that separated the pumping chamber from the crypt.

Colin looked over at the huddled form beside him. Deep, rhythmic snores told him Robin was still sound asleep. He reached across and nudged him. 'Robin! Come on, wake up.'

'What? Wassamarrer?' muttered Robin blearily.

'There's somebody out there.'

Robin glanced at the door. The light had stopped pulsing and everything was still.

'You're imaginng things. Go back to sleep.'

'I tell you I heard something!'

'Then go and sort it out. I need my sleep.' Robin disappeared inside the sleeping-bag.

Colin thought hard for a moment. He had seen something, he was sure of it. If he ignored it, it might well come back again, perhaps when he was asleep. Better to check up now.

Struggling out of his sleeping-bag, he hastily pulled on his boots and laced them with clumsy fingers. Reaching for the torch, he switched it on and headed for the door.

Cautiously he opened it, and shone his torch around the crypt. The torch-beam played over the faces of stone, the ornate tombs with their carved flowers and stone angels, and came to rest on a strange square structure. It was a kind of upright stone box, the general size and shape of a telephone kiosk. It stood on a stone dais, with four pillars, one at each corner. From the apex of each corner pillar, a hollow-eyed stone mask stared down.

The extraordinary thing was — it hadn't been there before.

In size and shape it was quite unlike any of the other tombs and Colin was sure he would have remembered it.

Suddenly a door slid upward, leaving a rectangle filled with light. Outlined in the doorway was a strange and terrifying figure. Roughly man-sized and man-shaped, it was a kind of giant walking lizard, thick-bodied with corrugated green skin and a narrow-skulled head that ended in a mouthful of jagged teeth. Its stubby hands held a strange light-filled weapon — which was trained on Colin.

As Colin cowered back, a beam of light sprang from the weapon. For a moment Colin's whole body flickered

15

between positive and negative. The glow flared brighter and Colin disappeared . . .

The Doctor opened his eyes and winced, rubbing his forehead. Nyssa was kneeling beside him.

'Thank goodness you're all right.'

He sat up looking around him. 'How long have I been like this?'

'Not long. What was that thing? It just appeared from nowhere.'

'Not from nowhere, Nyssa. From another dimension.'

'Has it gone?'

'From the TARDIS? Yes, I think so.'

'What a relief! For a moment, I thought it was taking you over.'

'For a moment it did. What you saw, Nyssa, was an attempted temporal bonding. The molecular realignment of two basically incompatible life-forms.'

'I checked the sensors while you were unconscious, Doctor.'

'And?'

'Only one thing could account for those readings. The creature is formed from anti-matter.'

'Then it's even worse than I thought.'

'But the creature failed, Doctor. It isn't in our dimension now.'

'I think it is — somewhere. And it's half-way to achieving its purpose. It won't give up that easily.'

Nyssa frowned. 'To remain in our Universe it would have to reverse its polarity. If it tried to do that and failed . . .'

'Matter and anti-matter in collision,' said the Doctor bleakly. 'Yes, I know. Come on, Nyssa, we've got work to do.'

The sudden flare of light from the doorway into the crypt forced Robin into wakefulness. He looked quickly at the sleeping-bag beside him. It was empty.

'Colin? Colin, where are you?'

Alarmed, Robin jumped out of bed. He put on his boots, fished a second torch out of his rucksack, and headed for the door to the crypt. Like Colin before him, he shone his torch around the crypt.

'Colin?' There was no answer. 'Okay, very funny,' said Robin nervously. 'Now cut it out. Come out and show yourself.'

There was no answer, only the eerie gurgling of the water pipes.

Robin waved his torch around the crypt, looking for his friend, and found instead the strange oblong stone structure. As his torch-beam struck the side, there came a strange high-pitched sound, and a door opened in the side.

Robin stared in horror as the strange lizard-like being stalked towards him – but he wasn't so terrified that he couldn't see that the thing was holding some kind of weapon. As the creature raised the weapon, Robin sprang to one side. The energy blast struck a stone angel, which flickered from positive to negative and disappeared.

Before the creature could fire again, Robin dived back into the pump house, closing the door and bolting it behind him.

The door shuddered as something heavy and powerful crashed against it. Robin ran to the far end of the pumping house, unbolted the service exit and dashed through, slamming it behind him.

In a council chamber on Gallifrey, the Castellan, Councillor Hedin and Cardinal Zorac, together with Chancellor Thalia, sat watching Lord President Borusa.

White-haired and aristocratic, President Borusa sat motionless on the elaborately decorated presidential chair. Inches above his head hovered the Matrix Crown, the incredibly complex device which linked him with that strange combination of group-mind and race-memory Time Lords called the Matrix. This kind of direct communication was both dangerous and stressful. It was only used in the gravest of emergencies.

President Borusa raised his head and opened his eyes. The Matrix Crown rose of its own accord, and hovered several feet above his head.

'Well, Lord President?' said Zorac. He was dark and thin-faced and always seemed aggrieved.

Borusa said heavily, 'The Matrix only confirms what we already know, Cardinal Zorac. The creature is highly intelligent, immensely powerful, and it is formed from anti-matter.'

'It's a damnable business,' said Zorac explosively. 'Damnable. Thalia, you're the expert on this sort of thing. What do you have to say?'

Chancellor Thalia, a handsome woman in the prime of life, thought for a moment before she replied. 'In theory, movement between dimensions is possible. In practice, rather less so. But then, the same thing was once said about time-travel and for us that has long been a reality.'

Councillor Hedin's long thin face was grave. 'Has the Matrix fixed the location of the creature?'

'Impossible,' said President Borusa. 'Temporal

distortion is extremely severe.'

'The creature must be shielded for the present,' said Thalia. 'But very soon the shielding will inevitably start to decay.'

'Then we shall know precisely where the creature is,' said Zorac grimly.

The Castellan, smooth-faced, blandly authoritative, spoke for the first time. 'By which time it will be too late.' He paused, and looked meaningfully round the group. 'Unless of course the bonding were to be severed.'

'That of course is quite another matter,' said Thalia sharply. 'We all know what that would mean for the Doctor.'

No one spoke, but they all knew what she meant.

There was only one safe and simple way to sever bonding of this kind – ensure that one of the parties to the bond was no longer alive.

3

Recall

Nyssa was reading from the data-blank screen on the TARDIS console. 'Rondel: an intergalactic region, devoid of all stellar activity. In former times, the location of collapsed Q star.' She looked up at the doctor. 'Q star?'

'They're very rare,' said the Doctor. 'Very rare indeed. On burn-out, a Q star creates Quad magnetism. That's probably what the sensors picked up. Quad magnetism is the only force with the ability to shield anti-matter.'

'Then that's what will be shielding that creature – the one that tried to take you over.'

'Has to be,' said the Doctor thoughtfully. 'But that kind of shielding is known to decay very rapidly. Anything else in the data banks?'

'Not much. Just the name the ancients gave to this region.'

'What name?'

'The Arc of Infinity!'

The Doctor rushed over to the data screen and studied it eagerly. 'That's it, Nyssa! That's how the creature came through. What we saw was the gateway to the dimensions. The Arc of Infinity.'

The Time Lord watched eagerly as his alien ally materialised in the now-familiar cone of light.

The alien spoke, his voice a laboured gasp. 'The bonding registered in the Matrix?'

'Very clearly.'

'And the High Council?'

'Had no choice but to act as we predicted. But what of you? I detect weakness.'

'That is my concern, Time Lord, not yours. Carry out my instructions and all will be well.'

Nyssa said thoughtfully, 'So if this creature can't complete its bond with you, Doctor, it can have no real existence in this Universe?'

'Exactly.'

'And to bond with you successfully, it would have to have detailed biological information?'

The Doctor nodded. 'My bio-data. Which exists only in the Matrix – on Gallifrey. Which means . . .'

Nyssa completed the sentence. 'Someone on Gallifrey passed it on.'

As usual, Damon was working in the computer room, though he was constantly distracted from his work by thoughts of Talor. His superior had been found by a fused console, apparently killed by a freak burn-out. When Damon had reported his suspicions to the Castellan, he had been ordered to take over Talor's duties as well as his own. When he had raised the question of the illegal transmission of the Doctor's bio-data, he had been brusquely told that the matter was 'in hand' and warned not to meddle with affairs that did not concern him.

Damon was both worried and afraid. He looked up

nervously as Commander Maxil strode into the computer room, a burly figure in shining breastplate, his helmet of office under his arm. He was followed by two armed guards. All three looked strangely incongruous in this peaceful setting.

Maxil thrust an embossed plastic data-card towards him. 'You are to feed this directly into the Matrix. Immediately.'

Damon stared at the card in astonishment.

'Well, get on with it,' snapped Maxil. 'Don't you recognise the Presidential Seal?'

'I will need to confirm your authorisation,' said Damon hesitantly.

Maxil nodded to the guards. 'Arrest him.'

'Please,' stammered Damon. 'Wait . . .'

Maxil held up his hand, checking the guards. 'The Presidential Seal is all the authorisation you need. To disobey is treason.'

'Perhaps I spoke in haste,' admitted Damon. He looked at the data strip. 'But to recall a TARDIS, without consent, without prior announcement! You must understand my position.' It was clear that Damon was thoroughly cowed.

Maxil waved away the guards and said more gently, 'Such a decision was not made without due and proper consideration. Just obey the instruction, Damon. I will take full responsibility.'

Damon moved to a seldom-used console, and slipped the data strip into the appopriate slot. There was an immediate hum of power as the recall programme was activated.

Damon turned to Maxil. 'When the TARDIS has been recalled, whereabouts on Galifrey do you want it located?'

'In the security compound – to which only I will be allowed access. My guards will be waiting outside. Inform them the moment the TARDIS arrives.'

Maxil turned and strode from the room, his guards at his heels. Worriedly, Damon looked after him, and then turned his attention back to the recall console. It was clear that matters of state security were involved here. There must be no slip-ups.

The Doctor and Nyssa were still discussing the astonishing events that had taken place in the TARDIS.

Nyssa looked up from the console. 'There was a massive energy transfer when it happened.'

The Doctor nodded. 'It would seem that this creature controls the shift of the Arc. Just think of it Nyssa: sufficient power to unlock the door to travel between the dimensions of matter and anti-matter.'

Suddenly a light began pulsing fiercely on the console – a light that Nyssa had never seen before. 'Doctor, we've changed course!'

The Doctor couldn't believe it. 'The recall circuit! It can only be activated by order of the High Council. We're being taken back to Gallifrey.'

Nyssa stared at him. 'Why?'

'I don't know. But it must be urgent. Very urgent. As far as I know, that recall circuit has only been used twice before in all Time Lord history.'

After his escape from the terrifying experience in the crypt, Robin had hung about the gardens of the old house until daylight, so shocked, he had been unable to move for hours. Only the early-morning arrival of a couple of gardeners had shaken him from his panic-stricken inertia. He had to hide in the shrubbery to avoid them, but somehow the sight of the familiar workaday figures had given him courage.

Desperately he tried to decide what to do next. Report matters to the authorities? No one was going to believe his story about the monstrous creature that had attacked him in the crypt. He'd just get himself put in a mental home, and that wouldn't help Colin.

The first thing to do, decided Robin, was to go back and look for Colin. He might still be hiding in there somewhere, wounded, too terrified to move.

Even though it was daylight, Robin was reluctant to return to the crypt. It took all his courage to force himself to move back along the tunnel and open the door that led into the pump house.

The little room was empty, quiet except for the steady humming of machinery and the gurgling of water in the pipes.

His rucksack and sleeping-bag were still there, just as he had left them. Hastily Robin repacked his belongings and slung the pack on his back. That done, he looked fearfully at the other door – the door that led to the crypt. He took a hesitant step towards it – but suddenly light flared through the gap beneath, and it started to open.

Robin dived for cover, concealing himself behind one of the banks of machinery. He heard the door to the crypt squeak open, and light spilled into the room. Cautiously Robin peered out from his hiding-place, and saw a familiar figure in jeans and anorak, attaching something to the pumping machinery. It was Colin.

Robin stepped out of hiding. 'Colin!' he called softly.

The figure froze for a moment, then went calmly on with its work.

'It's me, Colin,' whispered Robin. 'Come on, we've got to get out of here. I was thinking about getting the police, but they'd never believe us. Anyway, let's get away from this hell-hole.' He put his hand on Colin's shoulder. Colin turned, and Robin backed away, horrified.

Colin's face was a ghastly white, dead white, like that of a corpse. His red-rimmed eyes gazed straight ahead in a fixed stare.

Suddenly Robin heard movement through the open door to the crypt. Panic-stricken, he made a rush for the far door. Struggling with the weight of his heavy pack, Robin dashed along the service tunnel, through the door at the far end, and out into the blessed daylight.

The security compound was just that: an open space with thick walls and an impregnable door . . . It was empty – until there came a wheezing groaning sound and a TARDIS materialised in the centre. It was in the form of a police box, of the kind once used on Earth.

Its arrival was monitored by Damon in the computer room . . . and by Commander Maxil who appeared suddenly at his side.

'The TARDIS has arrived, then?'

'Yes, Commander. I was about to inform you.'

'Is the security compound sealed?'

Damon checked the remote-control circuit. 'Yes, Commander.'

'Excellent.'

Summoning up his courage, Damon said, 'Commander Maxil . . . *why* are you treating the Doctor like a criminal?'

'I am simply following my orders.' Maxil turned and strode from the room.

Damon stayed at the recall console, staring worriedly at the battered blue police box on his monitor screen.

The Doctor and Nyssa emerged from the TARDIS, looked around the featureless open space, and made for the only door.

'Where are we?' asked Nyssa.

'In a security compound, in the heart of the Citadel. They're not taking any chances.'

The Doctor tried the exit door. As he had expected, it was locked.

'We're locked in!' said Nyssa indignantly.

The Doctor examined the lock. 'Hand-print activated – from outside. That and remote control.' He looked thoughtfully at Nyssa. 'Fetch my ident kit from my workbench, will you? I might just be able to trip the lock. Quickly!'

Nyssa gave him an exasperated look and hurried off.

Tired and dispirited, Robin came into the reception area of the hostel. It was a clean, well-lighted place, but the pleasant friendly atmosphere did nothing to cheer him up. He had just spent a frustrating hour at the police station, trying to convince the benignly sceptical Dutch authorities that something terrible had happened to his friend Colin Frazer. Things hadn't been made any easier by the fact that his story was so vague. Even to convince the police, Robin simply couldn't bring himself to tell them what he had seen in the crypt. In fact, the whole thing had become such a nightmare that he wasn't really sure what he had seen himself.

Robin waited glumly until the receptionist, a cheerful, friendly, blonde Dutch girl with a pony-tail, finished dealing with another enquiry. 'You have a room booked for me, I think.'

Briskly the girl said, 'What name please?'

'Stuart. Robin Stuart.'

'How long will you be staying, Mr Stuart?'

'I don't really know. A few days, maybe.'

'No problem,' said the receptionist cheerfully. 'Just let us know when you want to leave.' She handed him a room key. 'You are in room 34.' As Robin started to leave she called out, 'One moment. You are the Mr Stuart who reserved at the same time as Mr Frazer? Mr Colin Frazer?'

'That's right.'

'Will Mr Frazer be checking in himself today?'

Robin had a quick vision of Colin's white face and staring eyes. 'Don't count on it!'

The girl looked puzzled. 'I do not understand what you mean.'

'What I said,' shouted Robin almost hysterically. 'Colin Frazer won't be coming here, not today and not tomorrow. If you want to know why, ask the police. They might even get around to looking for him – one day.'

Robin's outburst left the receptionist thoroughly confused. 'Something has happened to your friend? I am sorry. I only asked about him because there is a telephone message that is all.'

'Sorry,' said Robin awkwardly. 'What's the message?'

'His cousin will arrive at Schipol airport tomorrow morning at ten-thirty.'

This new problem was just too much for Robin to cope with. What on earth was he going to tell Colin's cousin? Deciding to leave the problem until tomorrow,

28

he went wearily up to his room.

The Doctor's ident kit was a small wallet full of electrically charged levers in various shapes and sizes, a sort of technological skeleton key.

It could deal with most locks, but not with the lock of a security compound on Gallifrey.

The Doctor sighed and straightened up, selected another lever, and set to work again.

Nyssa was still feeling indignant. 'I don't understand, Doctor. Why have we been locked in in the first place? Surely the Time Lords have brought you back to help find the anti-matter creature?'

'I wish I could believe that,' said the Doctor grimly.

'What other reason could there be?'

'It won't be that easy to track the creature down. The Universe is rather a big place, you know. However, there's a much simpler way to prevent the bonding.'

'How?'

The Doctor didn't reply. Nyssa stared at him in sudden horror. 'You mean – kill you? Is that why they've brought you back?'

'Possibly,' said the Doctor calmly, and went on with his work.

In the computer room, Damon had been watching the Doctor's struggle with the lock for some time.

Nerving himself to a decision, Damon reached out and flicked the remote-control switch.

Suddenly the door to the security compound clicked open.

'Doctor! You did it!' said Nyssa.

'On this type of lock – and so quickly? I doubt it.

Someone else took a hand. Come on.'

He led the way out of the compound and paused for a moment to check his bearings. 'This way!' They set off down the corridor.

A guard emerged from a room just behind them, and stared in astonishment at their retreating figures. Lifting his wrist-communicator to his lips he whispered, 'Commander Maxil?'

Not far away, Maxil and a squad of guards were marching towards the compound.

The guard's voice whispered from Maxil's communicator. 'Commander Maxil?'

Maxil raised his communicator. 'Yes?'

He listened in astonishment to the guard's brief message and turned to his men. 'This way. Quickly!'

'Where are we making for?' asked Nyssa.

'The computer room. Not far now.'

'Won't it be guarded?'

'It isn't usually. But now that they know we've arrived . . .'

They came to a corridor junction. 'Stay there while I check,' said the Doctor. He moved a little ahead – and a guard stepped from a room behind him, stasar levelled.

He was about to shoot, when Nyssa sprang forward and shoved him hard!

The guard staggered, the shot missed, and the Doctor dragged Nyssa around the next corner – only to find they were facing Maxil and more guards.

'Hello,' said the Doctor cheerfully. 'I'm the Doctor.'

Maxil raised his stasar pistol and shot him down.

4

Death Sentence

'No!' shouted Nyssa, but it was already too late.

'Take them away,' ordered Maxil coldly.

Two guards grabbed the wildly struggling Nyssa and hauled her off. Two more lifted the Doctor's body and carried it away.

In the council chamber, Zorac received a report of the incident on his wrist-communicator. 'Every time the Doctor returns to Gallifrey there is violence!'

'Perhaps it is we who should modify our approach,' suggested Hedin drily.

'The Doctor chose to resist the Capitol Guard.'

'Inevitably! We send armed guards when a friendly face and a welcoming hand would have sufficed. Is it any surprise that he resisted?'

The Doctor's body was carried into the TARDIS, and Nyssa was herded after him. 'He's hurt,' she protested. 'He needs proper medical attention.'

'He's stunned,' said Maxil callously. 'He'll recover.'

The unconscious Doctor was carried through the inner door. Maxil knelt and reached under the console, lifted an access hatch and removed a small but complex piece of circuitry. Immediately the ever-present low

31

hum of the TARDIS's power systems cut out. Only the lighting circuits remained in operation. Maxil turned to Nyssa. 'The compound will be guarded at all times. If the Doctor tries to leave again, my men will shoot to kill. See that the Doctor knows this.'

The guards returned through the inner door, and left the TARDIS.

With a last hard stare at Nyssa, Maxil followed them.

Nyssa turned and ran to find the Doctor.

The Castellan strode grim-faced into the council chamber. Immediately, an anxious group of Councillors gathered round him.

'Well?' demanded Thalia. 'Where is he?'

'The Doctor tried to evade security. Some force had to be used. He will be brought before you as soon as he is recovered.'

'The situation is critical, Castellan.'

'Of that, Lady Thalia, I am more than aware. If I may pass? I must give my report to the Lord President.' Brushing past Zorac, who was in his way, the Castellan made for the door that led to the presidential suite.

Nyssa's room in the TARDIS was small and simply furnished – a bed, a table and chair, a rack of clothes, a scattering of personal possessions. The Doctor was sitting on the bed, sipping a restorative cordial, while Nyssa looked on anxiously.

'How do you feel, Doctor?'

'Better thank you.' The Doctor rubbed his head. 'Not the most friendly of welcomes, though.'

'They've taken the main space/time element from the time-rotor.'

The Doctor smiled wryly. 'Naturally. That's the only

way to keep me and the TARDIS here.'

'What do we do now?'

'We need a link — something to prove there's a connection between this creature and Gallifrey.'

'And just how are we going to do that?'

The Doctor made no reply.

The doors to the presidential suite opened and the Castellan, more grim-faced than ever, marched out.

Maxil was waiting for him just outside the doors. The Castellan snapped, 'Maxil! The Doctor is securely held?'

'Yes, Castellan.'

'The High Council will want to see him as soon as he is fully recovered. And Maxil, see that he's there when he's sent for, or you'll answer to me.'

He marched off leaving Maxil glaring resentfully after him.

One thing was clear. The Castellan's interview with the President had not gone at all well.

A jet glided gracefully down onto Amsterdam's Schipol Airport, its slipstream ruffling the grass that surrounded the runway.

Inside the busy airport concourse a tannoy voice chanted: 'KLM announce the arrival of their delayed flight from London.'

Robin Stuart heaved himself wearily to his feet, checked an information monitor, and headed for the arrivals area.

In the computer room on Gallifrey, Damon was watching a print-out as it stuttered from a data bank. He kept glancing nervously at the doorway, as if he was doing something dangerous and forbidden.

When the print-out was complete, Damon ripped it from the feeder-slot, rolled it up tightly, thrust it into the pocket of his tunic and hurried from the room.

Robin Stuart waited in the arrival area until the passengers who had been met had gone off with friends and relatives, and the ones not expecting to be met had moved purposefully away in search of taxis or the airport bus.

Just one person was left, a small, slender girl with close-cropped auburn hair. She wore shorts, matching jacket, and a camisole top, and she was looking round as if she was expecting to be met and hadn't been.

This must be the one, decided Robin. He went up to her. 'Excuse me . . . Tegan Jovenka?'

She turned. 'Yes?'

Her voice had the same unmistakable Australian twang as Colin's. Robin felt a pang of discomfort at the incredible news he would have have to bring her.

'I'm Robin Stuart. I'm a friend of Colin's.'

Tegan held out her hand. 'Hullo. Colin told me you'd been travelling around together. Is he here?'

'I'm afraid not.'

'Is he all right?'

'Look,' said Robin awkwardly. 'Let's get into town, shall we, find a café. I'll tell you all about it there.'

The Doctor and Nyssa had just returned to the control room when the doors to the outside crashed open and Maxil marched in, flanked by stasar-carrying guards. 'You are to come with us, Doctor.'

The Doctor looked at the levelled weapons in mild surprise. 'There's really no need for all this fire-power.'

34

'My men have orders to shoot to kill at the slighest sign of resistance.'

'All right, all right. The council chamber, I suppose?'

'Yes.' With a wave of his stasar pistol, Maxil urged them forward.

'One moment,' said the Doctor. 'My companion is not involved in this matter.'

'I have orders to bring both of you,' said Maxil. 'Move!'

The Doctor and Nyssa were marched along the Capitol corridors. They passed through one of the recreation lounges, where one or two Time Lords sat on low chairs and couches, talking quietly. Damon was amongst them. He looked hard at the little procession, then rose and moved off casually in the same direction, the rolled-up data strip clenched tightly in his hand.

Tegan and Robin sat at a table in a café in the centre of Amsterdam. It was a big, bustling place, cheap and cheerful, much used by students and other young visitors to Amsterdam.

Tegan smiled at the waitress. 'Two coffees, please.' She turned to Robin. 'So, tell me, when did you last see Colin?'

'Well, it's difficult,' said Robin hesitantly.

'What do you mean, difficult?'

'It's very hard to explain. He's disappeared.'

Tegan stared at him. 'Disappeared? You mean he's just wandered off somewhere?'

Robin shook his head. 'It's more complicated than that.' He sighed. 'You're just not going to believe this . . .'

Haltingly, Robin launched into his incredible tale.

As the Doctor and Nyssa were brought to the council chamber, the murmuring group of Councillors broke apart and turned to face them.

Maxil and his guards bowed and withdrew.

They looked like rare exotic birds, thought Nyssa, their gorgeous robes forming and reforming in a swirl of colour.

The Doctor paused on the threshold with a nod of greeting. 'Councillors.' He was relaxed and confident, his manner that of one who greets his equals. With momentary surprise, Nyssa remembered that the unassuming figure beside her was of at least equal rank to any of the imposing Time Lords facing him. Indeed, for a while the Doctor had held the office of President, though only for a very short time and under extraordinary circumstances.

A Councillor in orange robes responded first to the Doctor's greeting. He had a long thin face, kindly and shrewd, though at that moment his expression was grave.

'Doctor! A great pleasure to see you again.'

The Doctor beamed. 'It's a pleasure to see you, Hedin. Nyssa, this is my old friend Councillor Hedin.' The Doctor looked round the group. 'Councillors, this is my companion, Nyssa of Traken.'

A handsome middle-aged woman in sumptuous white robes inclined her head graciously. 'You are welcome to Gallifrey, Nyssa of Traken. I am Chancellor Thalia.'

'Thank you,' said Nyssa formally.

A dark-faced, sharp-featured Councillor in purple robes came forward. 'Well, Doctor, an unpleasant business,' he said querulously. 'I'm sure you understand why the Lord President felt forced to recall you.'

'Not really. I would have returned willingly – given the opportunity.'

'Indeed, Doctor? You have not always been so co-operative in the past.' The speaker was a younger Councillor, gold-robed, with a chain of office around his neck. His manner was smooth and forceful, that of a man accustomed to being obeyed without question.

The Doctor turned towards him. 'Have I not, Castellan?'

Thalia said, 'If you remember Doctor, you were ordered to return Romana to Gallifrey. Yet you failed to do so.'

'Romana *chose* to remain in E-space,' said the Doctor unrepentantly.

Hastily Council Hedin said, 'Come, this is all past history.'

The Doctor nodded, rubbing his chest, still bruised by the stasar beam. 'Well, now that I am here ... Thalia, have you formed any theory about what has been happening?'

Evasively, Thalia said, 'There's been very little time, Doctor.'

The Doctor looked round impatiently. 'Has anyone checked to see if my bio-data extract has been removed from the Matrix? Castellan?'

'Exactly what are you suggesting, Doctor?'

'I should have thought that was obvious. None of this could have happened unless the alien creature had unlawful access to that information.'

'The most important thing at the moment, Doctor,' said the Castellan sharply, 'is to prevent –'

He broke off as an impressive figure entered the room, a medium-sized grey-haired man with an authoritative manner and fiercely intelligent eyes. He wore robes of silver, more elaborate than any of the others.

Zorac cleared his throat. 'Councillors – the Lord President,' he announced pompously.

The President stared searchingly at the Doctor for a moment. 'I see that you too have regenerated, Doctor.'

'Yes, indeed, President Borusa.'

'And this is Nyssa of Traken?'

President Borusa nodded graciously to Nyssa and then headed for the presidential chair, larger and more ornate than any of the others. 'I am sorry to have kept you all waiting. Please be seated, Councillors.'

The Councillors took their places, leaving Nyssa and the Doctor standing before them. Suddenly Nyssa felt isolated and very vulnerable.

His voice cold and formal, President Borusa said, 'This emergency session of the High Council is now in progress.'

Robin stumbled to the end of his story and looked despairingly at Tegan. 'Well, there it is. I don't suppose you believe a word of it?'

'Don't be so sure,' said Tegan. 'It sounds exactly like the sort of thing my friend the Doctor used to get me involved in.'

'The Doctor?'

'Someone I used to know. Have you reported any of this to the police?'

'Not all of it. How could I?'

'But you did tell them Colin has disappeared?'

'Sure.'

'What did they say?'

'Colin's a foreign national. Just another hitch-hiking teenager. Unless there's some evidence of violence –

38

foul play – they're not all that interested. It's the same everywhere.'

'Not interested!' said Tegan determinedly. 'We'll see about that!' Colin wasn't just another kid – he was Tegan Jovanka's cousin. 'We'll go back to the police together.'

Robin looked alarmed. 'I can't. I daren't get any more involved.'

Tegan looked angrily at him. 'What's that supposed to mean?'

'Look,' said Robin miserably. 'Everything I've told you is the truth. I swear it. But I've lost my passport. I can't risk making too much of a fuss with the police.'

Tegan sat back with a sigh, looking round the busy café. It was full of young people, all talking animatedly. Everyone seemed to be having a good time – except her. 'Marvellous, isn't it? First I lose my job. Not to worry, I think, I'll go and see my favourite cousin in Amsterdam and cheer myself up. Now this!'

'I'm sorry,' said Robin. 'I'm being selfish. Of course I'll help. What do you want to do?'

'Tell me your story again, every detail. Then we'll go to the police.' She caught Robin's look. 'Don't worry. It's all right. I'll do all the talking.'

The Lord President was addressing the High Council. 'In short, the space/time parameters of the Matrix have been invaded by a creature from the anti-matter world. We know its composition, we know how unstable must be the magnetism that shields it. The creature must be expelled immediately if we are to avert total disaster.'

'Shouldn't we at least attempt to discover its purpose here?' suggested the Doctor mildly.

'The removal of its presence must be our first and

only concern. Anti-matter cannot exist in harmony with our Universe.'

'I should like to raise another question, Lord President,' said the Doctor firmly. 'The creature is here now only because it managed to achieve some form of bonding with me. To do that it needed something very special – full and precise details of my biological make-up. In other words, my bio-data. Now, I didn't pass that information on, but somebody did. The question is – who?'

'You attempted to raise this matter earlier, Doctor,' said the Castellan coldly. 'What you imply is utterly preposterous.'

The Doctor turned to Thalia. 'You're the expert in this field. Can bonding occur without the full imprint of a bio-scan?'

'Not to my knowledge, Doctor,' admitted Thalia uneasily. 'But the power of this anti-matter creature may well be beyond the limits of what we know.'

The Doctor looked round in alarm. Why were they all so determined to ignore the obvious? There was a feeling almost of conspiracy. He raised his voice and said formally. 'Lord President, I insist that this matter be fully investigated.'

For a moment Borusa did not reply. He looked at the Doctor with a sort of stern compassion and suddenly the Doctor realised the reason for the evasiveness of the Councillors. This meeting was no more than a formality. The decision had already been taken. President Borusa's voice was grave. 'I am sorry, Doctor, but we must deal with the situation as it exists now. It is a matter of the utmost urgency, and the time factor leaves only one course of action open to us.' The President raised his voice. 'Commander Maxil!'

The Council Chamber doors opened, and Maxil entered flanked by three guards. All three had drawn stasar pistols in their hands.

Borusa said harshly, 'As I am sure you know, Doctor, any form of capital punishment has long been abolished here on Gallifrey. But in extreme cases, such as this, where the security of the State is involved, a Warrant of Termination can be issued. With the greatest reluctance, the High Council have decided to issue such a warrant in your case.'

The Doctor had just been condemned to death.

5

The Prisoner

It was clear that the President was under enormous strain, but his voice did not falter. Borusa had always been able to face the realities of power. 'Have you anything further to say, Doctor?'

'I have a great deal to say,' said the Doctor furiously. He took a step towards the presidential chair, and immediately two guards seized his arms.

It had taken a few moments for Nyssa to realise what was happening. 'You can't do this!' she cried. 'You must destroy the alien, not the Doctor.'

For the first time there was a note of anguish in Borusa's voice. 'Child! Do you think we have not considered this? The Universe is vast, and the creature is shielded. We have no way of tracing it!'

'So you're going to kill the Doctor instead, just because it's easier?'

'With the Doctor . . . terminated, the creature's link with our Universe will be broken, its plans, whatever they are, defeated. There is no alternative.' Borusa raised his voice. 'Commander! Return the Doctor to the security compound. As soon as the warrant is issued, you will convey him to the Place of Termination. I am sorry, Doctor.'

As the guards started to lead the Doctor away, Nyssa

sprang forward in protest. 'No, you can't. There must be some other way!'

One of the guards brushed her aside and the Doctor was marched to the door.

In the doorway the Doctor paused for a moment, looking back at President and the High Council. 'Executing me won't alter the facts, you know. There's a traitor at work on Gallifrey . . .' The Doctor's voice faded as he was dragged away.

Hovering nervously outside Amsterdam's Central Police Station, Robin looked up eagerly as Tegan came down the steps. 'What did they say?'

Tegan scowled. 'Foreigners get themselves lost all the time. They'll make routine enquiries at the house and the crypt. When they get around to it . . . which means, as you said, they'll do nothing!'

'What did you tell them – about the crypt.'

'Only that Colin was last seen there.'

'So what do we do now? We can't just abandon him.'

Tegan looked hard at him. 'You are telling me the truth about all this?'

'Yes, I am. I swear it.'

Tegan studied him for a moment longer, then said decisively, 'Right, then. Let's see if we can find Colin for ourselves!'

Nyssa was making a last desperate plea to the High Council. 'Time Lords, I beg you to think of what you are doing. The creature must have known the precise location of the Doctor's TARDIS, the complete time/space co-ordinates. It also had the Doctor's bio-data.' She looked round the impassive group. 'That information can only have come from here. From

Gallifrey.'

'Only a member of the High Council has the authority to extract such data from the Matrix,' said the Castellan coldly. 'Like the Doctor, you accuse us of treason.'

'Can you deny the possibility? At least give the Doctor a reprieve while the question is investigated.'

President Borusa said sternly. 'There is no time. Whether this charge is proved or disproved, it will not alter things. We must prevent the full bonding.'

'But the Doctor is innocent!'

'Innocence or guilt do not enter into the matter,' said Borusa sadly.

'What would you have us do, child?' demanded Thalia. 'If we spare the Doctor, we condemn untold millions to destruction. That is the choice we face here.'

Damon waited tensely as the Doctor and his escort neared the door to the security compound. By running through the corridors, Damon had managed to arrive ahead of them. Now everything depended on the way he handled this meeting. As the little party moved past him, Damon leapt forward, thrust his way through the astonished guards and clasped the Doctor warmly by the hand, shaking it vigorously. 'Doctor, it's you!'

'Damon, how are you?' said the Doctor, somewhat taken aback by the warmth of the greeting.

'Get him out of here,' ordered Maxil impatiently.

'I only want to speak to the Doctor,' protested Damon.

'What's wrong?' said the Doctor. 'He's an old friend of mine.'

'I have my orders,' said Maxil gruffly.

'Well, you don't have to relish them so much.'

Damon was bustled off, and the Doctor was marched on his way — clutching in his hand the rolled-up data strip Damon had thrust there during that first enthusiastic greeting.

Maxil opened the door to the security compound and the Doctor was thrust inside. They took him across to the TARDIS and Maxil opened the doors. Inside the control room the guards took positions by the doors, obviously prepared to stay.

The Doctor slipped the data-strip into his pocket. Somehow he had to find a way to be alone.

By now Nyssa had realised that she was talking to closed minds.

'I am sorry,' said Borusa finally. 'We have listened to what you say, we understand and we sympathise, but our decision must stand.'

Councillor Hedin said, 'Lord President, in view of Nyssa's most convincing arguments, could we not at least delay the execution?'

Borusa shook his head. 'I am sorry.'

Thalia said, 'We dare not take the risk, Hedin.'

Zorac added, 'We're all sorry, child, but there is really no other choice.'

'So much for Time Lord justice,' said Nyssa bitterly. She turned and left the council chamber.

The Castellan said briskly, 'All that remains is for the Warrant of Termination to be drawn up. The precise wording should be in the Matrix. I will see to it at once.'

'Whatever should we do without your diligence, Castellan?' said Hedin sadly.

Borusa rose. 'This session of the High Council is at an end.'

Nyssa was striding angrily away from the council chamber when she saw a young Gallifreyan in a brown tunic coming along the corridor towards her.

As they came level, he peered into her face. 'Nyssa? Nyssa of Traken?'

Nyssa stopped. 'That's right.'

'I am Damon. I'm a friend of the Doctor. We must talk.' He glanced round anxiously as a guard came along the corridor. 'Not here though. Come.' Taking Nyssa by the arm, he led her away.

The High Council merged from the council chamber, talking in low voices.

Hedin hurried to catch up with the Castellan. 'A moment, if you please, Castellan.'

'Well?'

'I cannot help being worried by what the Doctor and his companion said. Their allegations –'

'That there must be some connection between this creature and the High Council?'

'Precisely. The very suggestion that one of the High Council could be a traitor is extremely disturbing.' Hedin paused. 'Do you intend to pursue the matter?'

The Castellan shook his head dismissively. 'There is no real evidence. Not unnaturally, the Doctor and his companion were both overwrought.'

'All the same,' persisted Hedin. 'If it were true –'

'It is not true,' snapped the Castellan. 'Because if such a serious breach of security had occurred, I should know!'

Abruptly he turned away.

Damon took Nyssa to one of the recreation lounges. They sat at one of the low tables. A handful of

Gallifreyans sat talking at nearby tables, though none were close enough to overhear.

'You're sure it was the Doctor's bio-data extract?' whispered Nyssa.

Damon nodded. 'I managed to pass a copy to the Doctor on his way to the security compound.'

Nyssa started to rise. 'We must tell the High Council at once.'

Damon put a hand on her arm. 'Wait, Nyssa. Only members of the High Council have access to bio-data.'

'Which means that the traitor must be one of them,' said Nyssa slowly.

'That's right. So, how do we know whom to trust?'

Nyssa considered. 'We must find some way to speak to the Doctor.'

'That will be difficult. He's very closely confined.' Damon's face cleared. 'But I know someone who might help . . .'

The distorted negative manifestation of the anti-matter creature fluctuated eerily inside the cone of light. 'It is decided, then?'

'Yes,' said the Time Lord. 'The Doctor is to be terminated.'

'Excellent. You are prepared?'

'I am. The Matrix is already programmed.'

The glare faded, and the alien disappeared.

Watched by an impassive guard, the Doctor marched angrily up and down the TARDIS control room. After a moment Commander Maxil entered.

'You asked to see me, Doctor?'

'Yes. Your guards will not allow me to leave the control room.'

'They have their orders.'

'If I am to die,' said the Doctor levelly, 'I need time to prepare my mind – and for that I need to be alone.'

Maxil frowned. 'Which is the nearest room?'

'My companion's. It has already been searched.'

Maxil considered for a moment. 'Very well, Doctor, you may withdraw until it is time. But be sensible. If you try to lose yourself in the corridors of the TARDIS my men have detector devices that will hunt you down and your death will be far from dignified and painless.'

Without bothering to reply, the Doctor turned and left the control room.

Formal head-dress and high-collared robe removed, Councillor Hedin was relaxing in his room when Nyssa and Damon called to see him. He rose to receive them. Nyssa! Damon!'

'We had to see you, Councillor,' said Nyssa urgently. We need your help.'

Hedin sighed. 'I cannot tell you how deeply sorry I am for what has happened. If there is anything I can do or you . . .'

'We must see the Doctor. Can you arrange it?'

'It will be difficult. The Castellan is very possessive about his charges.'

'The Doctor isn't a criminal,' said Damon indignantly.

'That is true. But what has happened makes him very dangerous, and he will be well guarded.'

'Please try,' begged Nyssa.

Hedin's long, thin face broke into a gentle smile. 'I said difficult, Nyssa – but not impossible. Especially with one so sensitive to public opinion as the Castellan.'

For a moment Nyssa was puzzled. Then, with a chill

pang she realised what Hedin meant. The Castellan wouldn't want it said that the condemned man hadn't been shown every consideration – before his execution.

In a surprisingly short time, everything was arranged. Hedin went off to see the Castellan, and shortly afterwards Commander Maxil himself collected Damon and Nyssa from Hedin's room and marched them along to the security compound.

'Wait here,' he ordered, and went into the TARDIS.

'I think there's something wrong,' whispered Damon. 'The Castellan agreed far too quickly to our visiting the Doctor.'

'What do you mean?' asked Nyssa, concerned.

'Even if he knows he can't really refuse something, he always attempts to make it look as if he's granting you some enormous privilege. I mean, that's the Castellan's way –'

He broke off as Maxil appeared in the doorway of the TARDIS. 'Come along, you two!'

The Doctor was pacing about Nyssa's room, studying the bio-data read-out when the guard appeared. 'This way, Doctor.'

Hastily slipping the read-out into his pocket, the Doctor followed the guard along the corridor. 'So soon?' he demanded. 'What about my appeal?'

There was no reply.

'He's just coming,' said Maxil.

As Nyssa and Damon looked towards the inner door, Maxil took the opportunity to slip a magnetic bugging device beneath the TARDIS console.

The Doctor came into the room. 'Nyssa, Damon . . . how did you get in here?'

Nyssa said, 'We went to see Councillor Hedin, and he arranged it with the Castellan.'

'Well, that's very generous of the Castellan, isn't it? Come, let's talk in Nyssa's room.'

'Just a moment,' said Maxil, a little over-emphatically. 'You're to talk in here.'

'The Castellan said we could be alone,' said Damon, quite untruthfully.

Maxil hesitated and the Doctor said quickly, 'Excellent!' He bustled them out of the control room talking in a loud cheerful voice. 'Well, Damon, what news of my old companion, Leela?'

In his office, the Castellan listened to the Doctor's voice.

'How is she adjusting to life on Gallifrey?'

Then Damon. 'Oh, very well . . . she's very happy.'

The Doctor again. 'I was sorry to miss her wedding, but perhaps I may get to see her before I finally depart.'

The Castellan smiled wryly. It was clear that the Doctor knew, or at least suspected, about the bugging device. He would say nothing but conversational banalities until he was out of earshot. Maxil had bungled things somehow.

'You're a fool, Maxil,' said the Castellan irritably, and switched off the listening device.

The Doctor ushered his visitors into Nyssa's room. 'In here. I rather think Maxil has just planted a listening device in the control room.' He held out the bio-data print-out. 'My thanks, Damon. Now we have proof that my bio-data extract was removed from the files.'

'So there is a traitor after all?' said Nyssa.

'Indeed there is. And a disaster in the making. Unless

51

I'm very much mistaken, Gallifrey could lose control of the Matrix.'

Damon was shocked. 'Surely that's impossible?'

'That's exactly what the High Council thinks. We must see what we can do to stop it happening. I know you've already risked a great deal for me, but if I could impose on you even further?'

'Anything I can do, Doctor.'

'To begin with, I need another space/time element for the TARDIS. Preferably one without a recall circuit!'

'I'll see what I can manage. Anything else?'

'Yes. You could check to see if the Matrix is aware of any recent events concerning power equipment – movement details, transportation, anything you can find.'

'Right, Doctor.'

The door opened and Maxil marched into the room, glaring around suspiciously.

Before Maxil could speak the Doctor said, 'Is our time up so soon, Commander?' He looked at Nyssa and spoke with a complete change of tone. 'No, Nyssa, that is my final word. No appeals, no protests. We must accept the decision of the High Council. Is that understood?'

Nyssa gaped at him in utter astonishment.

6

Termination

Nyssa looked round the computer room, taking in the row upon row of data storage banks, and the ranks of terminals and control consoles. 'Very impressive.' Her eye wandered to a transparent wall-cabinet with a rack of stasar-pistols inside.

Damon said agitatedly, 'We must hurry. First I must check the coding for a Type 40 space/time element, then I must work out how I can draw one from technical stores.' He went to a nearby terminal and started punching controls.

Nyssa's eyes went back to the rack of stasar pistols. One thing she was sure of: whatever happened, she wasn't going to stand tamely by and watch the Doctor's execution.

Maxil was reporting to the Castellan in his office, a place as streamlined and functional as the Castellan himself.

'All is in order, Castellan.'

The Castellan rubbed his chin. 'No appeals? No last-minute requests?'

'No, sir. The Doctor seems to be taking it quite well, in fact.'

The Castellan looked thoughtfully at him. 'You

know, you are extremely privileged, Commander
Maxil. It is given to very few to supervise the
termination of a Time Lord ... It has in fact, only
happened once before.'

'Has the warrant been issued, Castellan?'

'It has. Summon the Doctor.'

The Doctor meanwhile sat brooding in Nyssa's room.
Surely his theory was right. It must be right.
Nevertheless, he was about to take a most desperate
gamble – with death the penalty of failure.

In the secret chamber beneath the Capitol, the alien
had materialised for a last conference with his Time
Lord confederate. 'Is it time?'

The Time Lord said solemnly. 'The Council has been
summoned to the Place of Termination. You have but
little time now. Can you do what is needed?'

'All will be ready here.'

The alien faded away.

In his own control room, the masked and cloaked figure
of the alien sat breathing hard for a moment, almost
exhausted by his efforts. He rose laboriously from his
high-backed chair as Colin appeared, escorted by the
hideous creature that had captured him.

The alien waved towards the black control console
that stood in the centre of the control room. 'Do
precisely as you have been instructed. To the controls.'

His face blank, his mind totally controlled, Colin
shuffled zombie-like to the console and stood waiting.

Nyssa watched as Damon assembled a variety of spare
parts into a new space/time element for the Doctor's

TARDIS. A deep, sonorous chime resounded through the computer room – a chime that would be heard throughout the Capitol.

Nyssa looked up. 'What is it?'

'The summons. The Doctor is being taken to the Place of Termination.' Damon looked up from his work despairingly. 'It's no good, Nyssa. We're too late.'

Nyssa jumped up. 'They're going to execute him now, right away?'

'Yes.'

Nyssa went over to the weapons rack and tried to open it, but it was locked. 'Damon, help me.'

'No, Nyssa. You can't stop them now.'

'*Help me!*'

'Please, Nyssa, listen to me. You'll die as well . . .'

'We can't fail the Doctor now, Damon. You finish assembling the element. But first, help me to get this open.'

Reluctantly Damon punched a code into the key panel at the base of the cabinet. The transparent cover slid back and Nyssa selected a stasar pistol.

'This is madness,' protested Damon.

Nyssa ignored him. 'As soon as you've finished you must get to the TARDIS and fit the element in place. They won't bother to guard it once the Doctor's gone. If all goes well, we'll need to leave in a hurry.' She moved towards the door.

'Be careful, Nyssa,' called Damon. 'And good luck.'

Concealing the pistol beneath her tunic, Nyssa hurried away.

The grave notes of the chime resounded through the Capitol as the Doctor was led in solemn procession to the Place of Termination.

55

Such Gallifreyans as they passed bowed their heads in sorrow — news of the doctor's arrival, arrest and imminent execution had spread rapidly through the Capitol.

Nyssa ran along the corridors, just in time to see the Doctor's party disappear around the corner. Cautiously she followed after them.

There was little enough to see in the Place of Termination. It was a plain, functional area, with metallic blue walls. In the centre was a kind of enclosure, defined by two semi-circular rails, a space just large enough for one man to stand. Above the enclosure was suspended a huge transparent tube.

Arrayed in their formal robes of office, the members of the High Council stood waiting.

The Doctor looked at each face in turn: Borusa, his face composed, showing little of the strain he must be feeling; Lady Thalia, sorrowful but determined; Zorac, tense and grim, nerving himself to an unpleasant duty; the Castellan, bland and impassive, as if Termination was an everyday event; and finally, Hedin, his face sad and solemn.

'Well,' said the Doctor grimly. 'I hope you know what you're doing.'

Borusa said gravely, 'You know the choice we have to face, Doctor. Your life, against the safety of the Universe. Our collective duty, if not our conscience, is clear.'

'Was the decision unanimous?'

'No. There was one dissenter. Your good friend Councillor Hedin.'

The Doctor smiled. 'Thank you, Hedin. I appreciate all you've tried to do for me.'

56

The Castellan handed the President a scroll. Borusa unrolled it and began reading aloud. 'By the authority vested in me, as laid down by Rassilon, I, Lord President Borusa, in accordance with the decision of the majority of the High Councillors here present, decree that this Warrant of Termination shall now be executed upon the Doctor . . .'

There were two guards posted outside the Termination Area. Nyssa paused for a moment. Reaching beneath her tunic she set her stasar pistol to stun, then began strolling innocently towards them.

She came closer, closer . . . Just as they were about to challenge her, she whipped out the pistol and shot them down, one after the other. Re-setting her stasar to kill, she slipped into the Place of Termination.

Borusa was concluding his speech. 'And so, by reason of cruel but unavoidable necessity, we have no option but to exercise the final sanction of Termination.' Rolling up the scroll, Borusa handed it to Maxil. 'Commander Maxil, this warrant empowers you to carry out our judgement.'

Maxil bowed his head respectfully, and took the scroll. 'Bring the Doctor forward.'

The Doctor was marched forward. He was just about to step into the Termination Area when Nyssa burst through the door, covering the tight little group with her stasar pistol.

The alien's control room was filled with a surging roar of power. Colin, reduced to no more than a pair of hands at the service of his captors, was busy at the controls.

'Align scan co-ordinates,' ordered the alien. Colin's

57

hands moved to obey.

'Over here, Doctor,' called Nyssa. 'Quickly.'

To her astonishment, the Doctor didn't move. 'No Nyssa. I will not have blood shed to save my life.'

'Guards, seize her,' ordered Borusa.

The guards moved forward.

Immediately Nyssa's weapon swung round to cove the President, and the guards froze.

'Nyssa of Traken,' said Borusa sternly. 'I comman you to lay aside that weapon.'

'Quickly, Doctor,' shouted Nyssa again.

'Obey the President, girl,' commanded Thali furiously. 'Otherwise you too will die.'

'You cannot escape, you know,' said the Castellan.

'Don't you understand?' said Nyssa desperately 'The Doctor was betrayed. His bio-scan was retrieved from the Matrix. Tell them, Doctor.'

'They're right, Nyssa,' said the Doctor calmly. 'W can't escape . . .'

'We can. We're all ready to leave!'

'Please, Nyssa, you must obey the Lord President. The Doctor held out his hand. 'Believe me, I know wha I'm doing!'

Nyssa was about to protest further when the Docto said firmly, 'The weapon, Nyssa, please.'

Nyssa lowered the stasar pistol. The Doctor took i from her hands and passed it to the nearest guard 'Lord President,' he said calmly. 'My companion acted solely from misguided loyalty. She will cause no furthe trouble. In return, I ask that she be allowed to go free.'

A little shakily Borusa said, 'Thank you, Doctor. Fo your sake, we will overlook her offence.'

Waving aside his guards, the Doctor walked over t

the Termination Enclosure and stepped between the two circular rails. He looked around the room and smiled reassuringly at Nyssa.

Borusa nodded to Commander Maxil, who threw a switch on the control panel.

The Enclosure filled with light, and the transparent tube of the Termination Chamber began lowering itself over the Doctor.

In the alien's control room, Colin stood waiting impassively as the power surged to its peak.

At last the order came. 'Activate booster control *now!*'

Colin threw a switch and the control room was filled with a blaze of light.

There was a blaze of light too inside the Termination Chamber, and a sudden swirling mist obscured the Doctor's form. Power hummed, the light blazed brighter, the mists boiled wildly. Watching in horrified fascination, Nyssa thought she saw just for a second the Doctor's figure fading and a strange alien shape taking its place. Then this shape faded too.

The power-throb died down, the light faded and the mist cleared from inside the Termination Chamber.

It was empty.

Commander Maxil bowed to President Borusa. 'Judgement has been carried out, Lord President. The Doctor is dead.'

Nyssa's eyes blurred with tears and she turned away.

7

The Matrix

President Borusa touched a control, and a large monitor screen lit up, high on the wall. It showed a symbolic representation of the Matrix, an interlocking web of energy impulses, a kind of three-dimensional spider's web.

Borusa studied the display. 'The Matrix is clear. The creature has been expelled . . .'

The Doctor awoke.

He was floating against velvet blackness . . . He felt weightless, almost disembodied. Was he dreaming? Periodically, energy impulses zipped past him at incredible speed – the speed of thought.

The Doctor opened his eyes and saw that he was floating in a great three-dimensional energy web, like a swimmer drifting gently with the tide. He was in the Matrix.

He heard soft, mocking laughter, felt some unseen, malignant presence.

'Who are you?' called the Doctor feebly.

There was no reply.

The Castellan strode away from the Place of Termination, Commander Maxil following respectfully at his heels.

The Castellan was silent, brooding. At last he said, 'What was your opinion, Maxil?'

'Of the termination, Castellan? Not quite what I expected.'

'Nor me. I want a full analysis of the event. Be discreet – but do it immediately.'

As soon as she'd recovered her self-control, Nyssa headed for the TARDIS. As she'd predicted earlier, it was unguarded now.

She found Damon in the control room. He had just completed the installation of the new space/time element. 'It's ready, Nyssa. We can leave – ' He broke off at the sight of her face. 'The Doctor? He's – '

Nyssa nodded. Too upset to speak, she went through the inner door.

The alien creature appeared in its cone of light. 'It is done.'

The waiting Time Lord leaned forward anxiously. 'And the Doctor?'

'Weak – but he lives. You have done well, Time Lord.'

Maxil came into the computer room. He looked round, relieved to find that for once the place was empty.

He went to a terminal and began punching in the programme for a full computer analysis of the Doctor's termination.

On a monitor screen in a room not far away a Time Lord was watching Maxil at his work.

Drifting, half-dreaming, the Doctor heard a deep, resonant voice. 'Doctor!'

He opened his eyes. There, floating somewhere in front of him was a masked, cloaked figure. The Doctor stared at it, trying to focus his eyes. The tight-fitting stylised mask resembled a knight's helmet, though more elongated, with something insect-like about it. The apparition wore a heavy medallion on its chest, like a badge of rank. There was something oddly familiar about it . . .

'Doctor!' called the voice again. 'Do you know where you are, Doctor?'

'The Matrix . . . I must be in the Matrix.'

'Only your mind. Your body is still in the Termination Area, shielded and made invisible by an energy barrier.'

The Doctor said weakly, 'I knew you wouldn't let me die.'

'You knew? You realised that this would happen?'

'I guessed. Besides, I hoped it would give me the chance to meet you.'

'And now that you have, what do you make of me, Doctor?'

'It's difficult to say – without knowing who you are. Yet you seem . . . familiar . . .'

Again there came the mocking laughter. 'Let us just say I am a friend, Doctor. A friend who holds your feeble life-force this side of existence.'

Robin led Tegan through the crowded centre of Amsterdam, down a series of quieter side-streets, and finally to a handsome old house set back from the road.

He took her through the entrance gates, and round the side of the house, the approach that led direct to the pump room. Not surprisingly, Robin didn't plan to go back into the crypt if he could possibly avoid it.

Tegan brushed dust from the shoulder of her jacket as they moved along the tunnel. 'It's filthy in here. What is this place?'

'It's a service tunnel. Not far now.' Robin opened the door, and led the way into the pump house.

Tegan looked round. There was nothing much to see. The horse-shoe shaped booster element which Colin had attached to the machinery was throbbing quietly, but neither Tegan nor Robin registered it.

'So this is where you slept?' asked Tegan.

'That's right. The crypt is through this door here.'

Tegan tried the door. 'It's locked.'

'Funny – it wasn't before. Maybe a gardener or caretaker's been down here.'

Tegan rattled at the door. 'For all we know, Colin could still be behind there. Maybe he's hurt.'

Something caught Robin's eye, a shape jammed behind one of the heavy pipes. 'Tegan, look!' He pulled out Colin's rucksack, which had been thrust into hiding. 'This is Colin's. He must be still around.'

Maxil scanned the data flowing across the read-out screen. He punched a re-play button, then studied it all again as if unable to believe his eyes.

He switched off the screen and spoke into his wrist-communicator. 'Castellan?'

'Yes, Maxil.'

'I think you should come down here at once, Castellan.'

'Very well.'

Maxil switched on the screen, and studied the data yet again.

64

The Doctor was still engaged in his strange dream-like conversation with the masked apparition. 'If you have something to say to the Time Lords, some proposition to offer them, why don't you speak to them directly?'

'I have considered that. But they would never listen. Not to me.'

'You are known on Gallifrey?'

'I was not always as you see me now, Doctor,' said the deep voice sadly. 'Once I too had life, real existence in your dimension. Soon, with your help, I shall have it again.'

'Not if it means losing control of the Matrix to you,' said the Doctor. 'The price is too high. The Time Lords would never permit it.'

'Do not provoke me, Doctor. We shall talk again — when you are more ready to listen.'

Exhausted by the effort of the conversation, the Doctor drifted back into unconsciousness.

The Castellan frowned down at the read-out screen.

'You see, Castellan,' said Maxil eagerly. 'I've been through the data again and again, and there can be no doubt. The circuit was altered, rigged to cut out at the moment of Termination.'

'Then the Doctor did not die!'

'Not according to this. And there's something else. The girl was right about the bio-scan. It was transmitted from here – on Gallifrey.'

In a nearby room, the watching Time Lord switched off his screen. It was time for action.

'We must find the Doctor,' said the Castellan determinedly. 'Do that, and the rest will fall into place.'

'Will you inform the High Council?'

'No. We will handle this ourselves, Maxil. Bring Damon and the girl Nyssa here to me.'

Robin and Tegan were still trying to decide on their next move. Tegan had been looking through Colin's rucksack, but had found nothing helpful.

'At least you know Colin was here now,' said Robin.

Tegan sighed. 'What beats me is why anyone would want to sleep in a place like this.'

Suddenly the pipes and the pumping machinery began throbbing with power. It sounded almost as if the water within was boiling.

They looked at each other in alarm. For a moment it seemed as if the whole system was about to explode. Then the sound steadied to a dull roar.

When Damon came into her room, Nyssa was sitting on the bed, staring blankly into nothingness.

'It's no use just brooding on things,' said Damon awkwardly.

There were sudden noises outside, shouts and the tramp of booted feet. The door opened and Maxil appeared, guards behind him.

Indignantly Nyssa jumped up. 'What are you doing here?'

'We've had orders to search the doctor's TARDIS.'

'What are you looking for?'

Instead of answering the question, Maxil said, 'You two are wanted. Come with me.'

'I demand to know what's going on,' began Nyssa.

Maxil drew his stasar pistol. 'Move!'

'Better do as he says, Nyssa,' said Damon wearily.

And Maxil marched them away.

Although they didn't know it, what Tegan and Robin were hearing was the operation of the newly installed booster element.

'What's going on?' asked Tegan again. 'It is all going to blow up?'

Robin shrugged. 'Search me. Maybe we'd better –'

Light flooded from beneath the door that led to the crypt.

'Quickly!' whispered Robin. Grabbing Tegan's hand, he dragged her into hiding behind one of the massive pipes that ran down the walls.

The door to the crypt creaked eerily open. Colin came into the pump room and moved past them, heading for the booster element.

Tegan tried to go to him, but Robin held her back. 'Wait!' he whispered.

Floating helplessly in the Matrix, the Doctor became dimly aware of some great disturbance. Something was happening, something very important. He had to . . . he had to . . . It was no use. He sank back into unconsciousness.

To Damon's surprise, Maxil took them back to the computer room, where a grim-faced Castellan was waiting by the data screen.

True to form, the Castellan began the conversation with an immediate accusation. 'Damon! You transmitted the Doctor's bio-data!'

Damon was shocked. 'No. Castellan, how could I? I do not have access to the necessary codes.'

'But you knew it had happened – this transmission?'

'Yes, Talor and I discovered it, more or less by accident.'

'Why didn't you tell me?'

'Talor tried to tell you,' said Damon angrily. 'You refused to see him. Next thing I knew, Talor was dead.'

Sternly the Castellan said, 'What are you implying Damon? Why didn't you come to me?'

'Only members of the High Council have the access codes to bio-scan circuits.'

'And so?'

'You too are a Councillor, Castellan. You see my dilemma?'

The Castellan changed his tack. 'There is another matter, even more serious. There was interference with the Termination Circuit.'

'Of that I know nothing, Castellan,' said Damon firmly. 'Once again, I simply don't have the authority to know the coding that would give access.'

'The Doctor would know. He could have instructed you. You had contact with the Doctor, did you not?'

'Yes, but that was only . . .'

Damon remembered that the reason he had made contact with the Doctor was to give him the read-out strip that confirmed that his bio-data had been illegally transmitted – not something he wanted to confess to the Castellan.

Damon was floundering hopelessly, when Nyssa came to his rescue. 'You're asking a lot of questions now, Castellan,' she said pointedly. 'It's a great pity you weren't more concerned when the Doctor was still alive.'

'Don't you play games with me, girl,' snarled the Castellan. 'The Doctor is alive – and you know it!'

8

The Traitor

Colin worked on the booster element for some time, while Robin and Tegan watched from their hiding-place. He seemed to be making a number of complex adjustments — which was ridiculous, Tegan realised suddenly. Her cousin Colin, who couldn't so much as change a light-bulb without making a mess of it, was operating some piece of complex alien machinery like a trained engineer.

Colin turned and Tegan saw the blank face and staring eyes, and realised that although the hands were Colin's, the mind behind them was not his own.

Colin finished his task and turned away.

Tegan could restrain herself no longer. 'Colin!' she called.

Colin ignored her. He walked stiffly out of the pump room and went back through the door that led to the crypt.

Tegan ran after him.

'No, don't!' called Robin.

'We can't just leave him,' said Tegan over her shoulder, as she followed Colin into the crypt.

On the threshold of the crypt, she stopped in horror. A door stood open in one of the tombs, giving forth a blaze of light. In front of it, facing her, stood Colin.

Beside him stood a hideous lizard-like creature with a long thin skull, ending in a mouthful of fangs. It held some kind of weapon in its hands.

Before Tegan could move, the weapon fired, projecting a fierce beam of light that struck and enveloped her.

From the doorway, Robin saw Tegan flash from positive to negative and disappear.

He turned to run, but it was too late. The creature fired again, and like Tegan, Robin pulsed from positive to negative and vanished.

The Doctor struggled to wakefulness. Something was happening, some great disturbance in the Matrix. He had to know. 'All right,' he shouted. 'All right, you win. Let's talk!'

There was no reply.

'We know there is a conspiracy,' said the Castellan. 'I am determined to get to the bottom of it.'

'You could start by finding the Time Lord who killed Talor,' said Damon boldly.

'We will. And we shall find the Doctor as well. Commander Maxil, mount a full search. He must be somewhere in the Capitol.'

Maxil saluted and stamped out.

The Castellan looked broodingly at Nyssa and Damon. 'I haven't finished with you two. You will remain here till I return!'

He strode out after Maxil, leaving a guard outside the door.

Nyssa grabbed Damon by the shoulders. 'He's alive, Damon. He's alive!'

Gently Damon disengaged himself and went over to

70

one of the computer termnals.

Nyssa watched him, puzzled. 'What are you doing?'

'I may have to stay here, but I don't have to stay here and do nothing. I'm not leaving everything to the Castellan either. I'm going to do a little investigating of my own.'

Commander Maxil surveyed the assembled squad of guards. 'Start by searching the residential wing, but be discreet. No one is to know we're looking for the Doctor.'

The guards moved away.

Tegan and Robin recovered, to find themselves in a featureless ante-room in front of a closed door.

Tegan rubbed her eyes. 'Where are we, Robin?'

'No idea. Do you feel all right?'

'I think so. A bit woozy.'

The door opened and a tall figure appeared. It was cloaked and masked, and it looked both powerful and sinister.

'Do not be afraid. If you co-operate you will come to no further harm.'

'Co-operate?' asked Tegan unsteadily. 'Why? What do you want of us?'

'To begin with – answers. Why did you intrude in a place where you had no business?'

'We were looking for Colin, my cousin.'

'I see. The primitive.'

The contempt in his tone made Tegan angry, and she forgot her fear. 'His name is Colin Frazer. He's my cousin. Where is he?'

The alien gestured towards the doorway. 'He serves me, in there. If you are capable of doing the same, you

71

will not find me ungrateful.'

'And if we're no use to you?'

'You will be destroyed.' The alien stepped aside, and the lizard-like creature appeared. 'The Ergon will scan you for possible future use. Step forward, girl. It would be unwise to resist.'

Tegan forced herself to move forward, and to stand quite still as the Ergon put a stubby clawed hand on her head. She felt a brief, tingling sensation and realised that in some way knowledge was being gathered from her mind and transferred, via the Ergon, to the mind of the alien.

The process took only a few moments. When it was concluded the alien said, 'So, you are known to the Doctor?'

'And if I am?' asked Tegan defiantly.

'Answer!'

'All right, I know the Doctor. I'm a friend of his. What of it?'

There was grim amusement in the alien's voice. 'Then we are both fortunate. It seems you can be useful to me after all.'

A steady beeping sound came from the door, and the alien turned and stalked away. His Time Lord confederate was summoning him.

As soon as the alien figure appeared in the cone of light, the Time Lord leaned forward urgently. 'There is trouble, grave trouble. A full-scale security search is in progress for the Doctor. They know he's alive.'

'How did this happen?'

'The termination aroused suspicion in some way. The Castellan investigated. He hasn't told the High Council yet – we must act before he does.'

'How shall we act?'

'Release the Doctor. He has to be free, here on Gallifrey, before you can concentrate your powers on transfer and complete the bonding. As a prisoner in the Matrix he is useless to you.'

'We cannot take the risk. Once free, the Doctor will make trouble.'

'We must take the risk. Your only hope now is to achieve transfer swiftly.'

The alien considered. 'As it happens, there may be a way that the Doctor can be persuaded not to interfere. Very well, Time Lord, I will do as you suggest.'

A voice spoke to the Doctor in the Matrix. 'Doctor.'

He opened his eyes and saw the masked figure floating before him. 'What do you want?'

'I have good news for you, Doctor. Since I wish for no enmity between us. I intend to release you.'

'Very good of you, May I ask what I've done to deserve it? Or should I say, what do you want in return?'

'You will be freed – if you give me your word not to interfere with my plans.'

'I will do everything I can to stop you,' said the Doctor steadily.

'Then I am forced to persuade you.'

Tegan appeared, floating in the Matrix.

'A friend of yours, Doctor. You will give me your word not to interfere – or she must suffer.'

'No. It's an illusion. It's not Tegan.'

'Tell him, girl.'

Tegan had suddenly found herself floating in this terrible limbo and she was very frightened. 'Help me, Doctor. Help me, please.'

73

'It isn't Tegan,' repeated the Doctor stubbornly. 'Tegan's on Earth, I know she is.'

'Very well, Doctor,' thundered the alien voice. 'If she is only an illusion, then you will not be distressed to see her suffer.'

Tegan's shape seemed to twist and distort, as if under intolerable pressure. She screamed, 'Doctor, *please!* Help me . . .'

The Castellan strode back into the computer room to find Damon running a computer programme. 'You! What are you doing?'

'An analysis. It is almost finished now,' said Damon calmly. 'I'll need your palm-print. The final results are classified.' He pointed to an illuminated square on the console. 'Just here, please.'

Too astonished to protest, the Castellan put his palm on the light-square. Immediately a stream of print-out came from a data slot. Damon took it out, scanned it swiftly and passed it to the Castellan.

As the Castellan took in the contents his face became grim and determined. 'I see. Well done, Damon.' He spoke into his wrist-communicator. 'Maxil!'

'Yes, Castellan?'

'Have you found him yet?'

'Not yet, Castellan.'

'Continue the search – and bring Councillors Thalia, Hedin and Zorac to my office – immediately.'

Damon said soberly. 'So now you know who is responsible, Castellan.'

'Yes. This analysis gives us all the proof we need.'

'So the Doctor is innocent!' said Nyssa triumphantly.

'Not necessarily. I believe that the Doctor plotted this conspiracy. Now I know who helped him to do it.'

The Castellan strode out closing the door firmly behind him. This time there was a sinister click.

Nyssa tried the door and found it was immovable. 'We can't get out.'

'No,' said Damon calmly. 'The Castellan has locked us in.' He returned to his console.

The Doctor was unable to stand the sight of Tegan's agony any longer. 'All right,' he shouted. 'All right, I'll do whatever you say.'

Tegan's image faded.

'Her life depends on you, Doctor,' warned the alien.

'As yours depends on mine?'

'Then see that nothing threatens it. Goodbye, Doctor. The next time we meet it will be on Gallifrey.'

The image of the Doctor faded from the Matrix.

When Tegan recovered consciousness, Robin was shaking her shoulder. 'Tegan! Are you all right?'

Tegan came to and found herself back in the anteroom. Robin looked anxiously at her. 'That thing put you into some kind of trance . . . What happened?'

'I'm not sure,' said Tegan. 'But I saw the Doctor . . .'

The Termination Chamber filled with light – and the Doctor materialised. The Chamber rose, and the Doctor was free again. He looked round cautiously. Luckily, the Place of Termination was empty.

He crossed to the door and looked out. The corridor beyond was empty as well. The Doctor hurried away.

The cloaked figure appeared in the doorway. 'Girl, you were of great help to me. To show my appreciation I return your cousin to you. I have restored his mind.'

To Tegan's delight, Colin came into the ante-room. He looked dazed and confused, but the ghastly fixed stare and the shambling zombie-like movements were gone. He stared disbelievingly at her. 'Tegan?' Before Tegan could answer he went limp and collapsed.

Tegan was just in time to catch him as he fell.

An angry little group of Councillors was gathered in the office of the Castellan.

Cardinal Zorac led the protest. 'What the devil is going on, Castellan? Guards crashing about everywhere, searches ... It's like a madhouse out there.'

The Castellan took his seat, and gestured to the rest of them to be seated. 'My apologies, Councillors.'

'So I should think!' said Thalia indignantly. 'We are not in the habit of being summoned by armed soldiers. We await your explanation, Castellan.'

The Castellan paused for a moment before he replied. 'An extremely grave situation has come to light. To begin with, I have indisputable evidence that the Doctor is still alive.'

'Ridiculous,' snapped Zorac. 'We saw him terminated.'

'The Doctor lives, Zorac. My men are searching for him now.'

Thalia said, 'How can he be alive?'

'He was helped to evade termination – by a member of the High Council.'

There was an astonished silence, during which Maxil entered with a sheaf of documents.

The Castellan said, 'Damon made an analysis of all the relevant security circuit traffic. I have had copies transcribed for you.'

As Maxil passed the documents round, the Castellan continued, 'Study them well, Councillors. They will tell you the name of our traitor.'

The Doctor made his way to the computer room in search of Damon and Nyssa, eluding several parties of guards on the way. He reached the door, only to find it locked.

The Doctor put his palm to the light square but nothing happened. 'Cancelled my authorisation long ago, I imagine. Pity.' He had a sudden brainwave. 'The presidential codes!'

The presidential codes cancelled all prohibitions, over-rode all other instructions. The Doctor began stabbing frantically at the keyboard beneath the lock. 'Let me see. Four . . . five . . . four . . . four . . . five . . . five.' He could hear booted footsteps in a nearby corridor. More guards! 'Three . . . nine . . . one . . . three . . . nine . . . one . . . three . . . nine . . .' The footsteps were coming closer. 'One . . . six . . . five . . . two!'

The door slid open and the Doctor slipped inside.

Damon and Nyssa stared at him in amazement, and then Nyssa ran to hug him. 'Doctor!'

'How did you open the door?' asked Damon.

The Doctor beamed. 'Pure luck!'

Thalia looked up from the documents in sheer astonishment. 'This is unbelievable, Castellan.'

'Nevertheless, Thalia, you hold the proof in your hands. The traitor is Lord President Borusa.'

9

Unmasked

'The Lord President?' said Thalia incredulously. 'Are you sure, Castellan?'

'His presidential codes were used to manipulate the Matrix. His code was registered in the computer room at the time Talor was killed.'

'But why?' demanded Zorac. 'Why would he do all this?'

By now the Castellan had worked the matter out – to his own satisfaction at least. 'The anti-matter creature. As you know, its link is with the Doctor and through him to Gallifrey. The President is allied with them both.'

'For what purpose, Castellan?' asked Thalia. 'What do they hope to achieve?'

'We know that the creature controls the shift of the Arc of Infinity. What if the Arc were to be located here, permanently, linked to the Matrix?' There was silence while the Councillors grappled with the idea.

The Castellan answered his own question. 'Power! Enormous power, well beyond the ability of anyone to control – *except for those who were already linked to the Matrix.*'

Zorac said slowly, 'The Lord President, you mean?'

'Yes,' snapped the Castellan. 'Through the Doctor

and this creature – I am convinced that this is precisely what they intend to do.'

'You might at least have told me what you were up to, Doctor. I thought you were dead.'

The Doctor said apologetically. 'I'm sorry, Nyssa, there just wasn't the opportunity. We were watched all the time remember. Damon, did you do as I asked?'

'I got you the space/time element, yes. It's already installed in the TARDIS.'

'What about the check on the movement of power equipment? Anything turn up?'

'Just one item, Doctor. A fusion booster element was transported very recently.'

'A fusion booster?'

'Apparently it's a very advanced piece of equipment still in the experimental stage. Unstable, but capable of an enormous conversion-rate over a very short period.'

'Conversion from what?'

'It's fuelled by anything that contains hydrogen atoms. Water would be perfect.'

The Doctor said urgently. 'Now listen, Damon, this is very important. I need to know the precise destination of that power booster. Where it was sent to and who sent it there. Do you think you could find that out for me?'

'I'll try.' Damon moved over to the computer console and set to work.

'Shouldn't we just go, while we've got the chance?' suggested Nyssa.

'We are going, Nyssa. We're going to Earth.'

'To Earth? What for?'

'That's where the anti-matter creature is now.'

'How do you know?'

'Tegan's on Earth, and the creature's got Tegan. I saw her, in the Matrix.'

The corridors of the Capitol were still busy with the bustle of armed guards – the Castellan was checking up on the progress of the search for the Doctor.

'The residential wings are cleared,' reported Maxil. 'My men are searching the technical areas.'

'You have sealed the Capitol?'

'Yes, Castellan. Nothing can get in or out without our knowing.'

'Then it's just a question of time, isn't it?'

The Time Lord and the alien were in urgent conference. 'The Castellan is very close to the truth now. Soon he will know everything . . . and so will the High Council.'

'They will take action,' said the alien slowly.

'Yes, but not until they find the Doctor.'

'You must delay them. I need more time if I am to generate sufficient power for transfer.'

'More time? I'll try, but I can't guarantee it.'

'You must! You will have to isolate the Matrix Master Control.'

'How?'

'Use your influence with the Lord President.'

'Very well. I will do my best.'

'Thank you, Time Lord.'

The Time Lord said, 'What we are, we owe to you. Your return is all that matters.'

The alien bowed his head, accepting the tribute as no more than his due. 'Very well. Meanwhile, I will try to prevent them using the Matrix against us.'

The alien faded away.

Councillor Hedin sighed deeply. Reaching into a

drawer, he took out the stubby impulse-laser with which he had killed Talor. Hedin hated violence, but any means – any means at all – were justified by the importance of the great cause he served. Concealing the weapon beneath his robes, Councillor Hedin, that gentle scholarly man who was also a traitor and a renegade, went out of the hidden chamber.

Tegan, Robin and Colin were still prisoners in the same featureless ante-chamber. Colin had recovered from his faint, but although more or less himself again, he seemed dangerously weak and confused. He had only the vaguest idea of what had happened to him, and had relapsed into an exhausted sleep.

More to pass the time than because they thought it would be of any real use, Robin and Tegan had been looking for a way of escape, but without success. The walls were impregnable and there was nothing to attack them with anyway. The only door led to the inner control room – from which their captors might emerge any moment.

Robin shook his head. 'There's no way out.'

'We'll just have to rely on the Doctor,' said Tegan cheerfully, though she spoke a good deal more optimistically than she felt.

'Your mysterious friend the Doctor? What can he do, he doesn't know where we are.'

'He knows that creature's captured me. He'll find out where we are – and he'll find some way to help us.'

Damon looked up from his data screen. 'I've found out what you wanted to know, Doctor. The fusion booster was transported to Earth.'

The Doctor came over to join him at the console.

'Well done, Damon. Any idea where?'

Damon shrugged. 'It could have been anywhere. The reception area was lost in severe spatio/temporal distortion.'

The Doctor stared at the screen. 'Pity.'

'I can tell you who sent it though.' Damon nodded towards the screen. 'You can see for yourself. Those codes are unmistakable. You used them yourself to get in here.'

The Doctor looked at the screen. 'The presidential codes!'

'That's right. There's other evidence as well. The Castellan is convinced Borusa's behind everything.'

'That's ridiculous! Come on Nyssa. We must see the Lord President immediately.'

'It won't be easy,' warned Damon. 'The Castellan's guards are all over the place.'

The Doctor clapped him on the shoulder. 'Thank you for all your help, Damon. I shall never be able to repay you.'

Nyssa went over to the weapons rack and got down another stasar pistol.

The Doctor was shocked. 'Nyssa!'

'Just in case,' said Nyssa unrepentantly. 'Don't worry, I'll set it on stun.'

The Doctor opened the door, peered into the corridor, waved farewell to Damon, and beckoned Nyssa to follow him.

'Goodbye,' called Damon softly. 'And good luck!'

The Doctor and Nyssa slipped away.

The square-jawed features of Maxil appeared on the screen in the Castellan's office. 'You wished to know if any of the High Council attempted to see the Lord

President, Castellan.'

'Get on with it, man.'

'Councillor Hedin is with him now.'

'Thank you, Maxil,' said the Castellan coldly. Maxil's face disappeared.

His face tight with anger and tension, the Castellan touched a control. The face of Lady Thalia appeared on screen. 'Yes, Castellan?'

'I have just been informed that Councillor Hedin has gone to see the President. We must act now, Thalia – if only to protect poor old Hedin.'

The Doctor and Nyssa were moving cautiously along the corridors when they were spotted by a patrolling guard.

The guard raised his stasar and fired. The stasar bolt whizzed past their heads, and the Doctor and Nyssa turned and ran.

The guard hurried to a wall panel, and soon an alarm beep was sounding through the corridors.

Maxil and a squad of guards heard it, not far away. 'Someone's spotted them,' shouted Maxil, and he led his men in the direction of the sound.

Meanwhile the Doctor and Nyssa were headed off by yet another guard. This time Nyssa was ready. Before the guard could even raise his stasar she shot him down.

They ran on past the stunned guard.

The Doctor spotted an open door. 'In here!' He pulled Nyssa after him.

Seconds later, Maxil and his men came thundering along the corridor, spotted the stunned guard, and charged on past. Not unnaturally, they failed to find the Doctor. Instead, they ran into the Castellan, approaching with yet more guards. 'Did you find him?'

'Not yet, Castellan. But he was spotted in the area, and he's stunned a guard. He can't be far away.'

'Hurry, Maxil, hurry. I need the Doctor. Find him!'

As soon as the corridor was clear, the Doctor and Nyssa emerged from their hiding-place, a conveniently empty office, and hurried on their way.

President Borusa studied his visitor thoughtfully, wondering why the calm and gentle Hedin was in a state of such agitation. 'This is a highly unusual request, Councillor Hedin. To isolate the Matrix!'

'It would affect only the Master Control. The secondary functions would continue to operate normally.'

Borusa was far from convinced. 'If I charge the transduction field, Hedin, the Matrix will be isolated. No one will be able to use it.'

'That is why you must do it, Lord President.'

President Borusa was not accustomed to being given orders. 'Must? You forget yourself, Hedin. Access to the Matrix is guaranteed. Not even the gravest of emergencies could induce me to do as you ask.'

There was a sort of gentle obstinacy in Hedin's voice. 'Nevertheless, Lord President, you *will* do it.' He produced the impulse-laser from beneath his robes and trained it on the President. 'Don't force me to use this.' He gestured towards the Master Control console in the corner of Borusa's office. 'Now, if you please, Lord President?'

The Doctor and Nyssa made it the rest of the way to the presidential chambers undetected – or almost. They were spotted by a guard just as they went through the door. As they came into Borusa's office, the Doctor was astonished to find their old friend Hedin covering the President with a hand-blaster.

'Why, Hedin?' Borusa was asking. 'Why are you doing this?'

Hedin whirled round as the Doctor and Nyssa entered.

For once, the Doctor jumped to the wrong conclusion, assuming that Hedin too had heard of the evidence against Borusa. 'Come now, Hedin, you don't really believe all this nonsense about the Lord President – ' He broke off, realising that the blaster was now trained on him. 'Hedin, what is it? What's going on?'

'Be careful, Doctor,' warned Borusa. 'Hedin is the traitor.'

Keeping the weapon trained on the Doctor, Hedin said. 'Throw down the weapon, Nyssa.'

The Doctor could scarcely believe what was happening. 'So it's you, Hedin. It was you all the time?'

'Nyssa, the weapon,' snapped Hedin.

Nyssa tossed the stasar to the floor.

Sadly the Doctor shook his head. 'The bio-scan, the rigged termination, all your work?'

'I did what I had to do, Doctor.'

'Taking care to arrange matters so that we should think the Lord President was responsible. What's your next move, Hedin?'

'To ensure that nothing interferes with the final bonding and transfer.'

'It's that close?'

'It is, Doctor. Very close indeed.'

'You know Hedin, I always considered you a friend. A historian, a man of learning, respected by everyone. Why turn to evil now?'

'You don't understand, Doctor. No one does – yet.'

'This alien creature will soon control the Matrix, Hedin. Is that really what you want?'

Hedin said fiercely, 'The creature as you call it, is no alien. It is one of us – a Time Lord. The first and greatest of us all. The one who sacrificed everything to give us mastery of time and space – and was shamefully abandoned in return.'

All at once, the Doctor realised what Hedin was saying. *Omega?*

'Yes, Omega!'

'But Omega was destroyed.'

No one knew that better than the Doctor himself. He had been there when it happened.

Omega, first and greatest of the Time Lords, the great cosmic engineer who had master-minded the incredibly dangerous black-hole experiment which had given his people time-travel.

In the process he had become trapped in a universe of anti-matter. Trapped, and in his own mind, abandoned by his people.

Omega had already made one attempt to gain his revenge – an attempt which it had taken no less than three combined incarnations of the Doctor to defeat.

'Omega was not destroyed,' said Hedin triumphantly. 'In his own anti-matter universe he is virtually indestructible. Omega exists. He only wants to return to our Universe, to live amongst us.'

'Hedin, you must listen to me,' said the Doctor desperately. 'No one is denying Omega's greatness, but you don't know him as I do. Long ages of suffering have driven him insane. Once in control of the Matrix, there's no telling what he'll do.'

'He wants nothing for himself,' said Hedin simply. 'The power he brings will be used for the good of all.'

It was easy to see what had happened, thought the Doctor. Hedin had always been obsessed with the early days of Time Lord history, the glories of the past. Contact with Omega had turned him into an unthinking disciple.

Suddenly the Castellan strode into the room, stasar in his hand and guards at his heels.

He glanced round, taking in the extraordinary scene. Then, like the Doctor before him, he misinterpreted the situation completely. Swinging his weapon to cover the Doctor, the Castellan said, 'Well done, Hedin.'

Borusa stared at him. 'Castellan, you fail to understand –'

'Lord President, I understand very well. You are under arrest. As for you, Doctor, you have already been condemned to death. This time there will be no trickery. I shall carry out the sentence myself.'

As the Castellan fired, Hedin performed his last service for Omega. With the Doctor dead, Omega would be unable to complete the bonding, unable to gain entry to the real Universe. Instinctively, Hedin threw himself in front of the Doctor, taking the full impulse of the stasar-blast on his body. The Castellan's stasar had been set to kill.

Hedin staggered back and crumpled to the floor, dying instantly.

Grieved as he was at the death of his old friend, there were more urgent matters on the Doctor's mind. 'Congratulations, Castellan. You've just killed the one person who could have told us where Omega is.'

'Omega?'

'Put up your weapon, Castellan,' said Borusa wearily.

By now the Castellan's assurance was shaken. 'But

the Doctor is a traitor. You are both traitors.'

Borusa pointed to Hedin's body. 'There is your traitor.'

'Hedin?'

'Lord President,' said the Doctor urgently. 'We must close down the Matrix.'

'Will that prevent transfer?'

'No, it's too late for that. But it will delay it, and give me time to find Omega.'

High on the wall of Borusa's office there was a Matrix screen. All the time they were there, it had been showing the intricate three-dimensional spider's web that represented the Matrix in its normal state.

Now Nyssa was staring at it in sudden horror. 'Doctor, look!'

The negative image of a masked cloaked figure was staring down at them from the screen.

'We're too late,' said the Doctor defeatedly. 'Omega controls the Matrix.'

10

Hunt for Omega

The doctor looked up at the terrifying form. 'Greetings, Omega.'

'You know who I am?'

'I do.'

'No matter, it changes nothing. Transfer will take place as I have planned.'

Borusa said, 'But how? You are anti-matter. You cannot exist in our Universe.'

'Omega, do you seriously believe you can reverse what has happened to you?' asked the Doctor.

'Oh yes, Doctor.'

'Not without Hedin's help,' said Borusa defiantly. 'Your confederate is dead, Omega.'

Omega's image seemed to grow brighter, as if burning with anger.

'Omega, listen!' called the Doctor. But it was too late. The screen flared white, and Omega disappeared.

'He must be found,' said Borusa. 'Found and stopped. Do you have any idea of his whereabouts, Doctor?'

'Only that he is somewhere on the planet Earth. When I was in the Matrix I learned he was holding a friend of mine captive – a girl from earth, called Tegan.'

'Perhaps she would know their precise location?'

'Possibly.' The Doctor looked hard at Borusa. 'But I would have to enter the Matrix to find out.'

Nyssa was horrified. 'No, Doctor, you mustn't. You said yourself, Omega's mad. He'll kill her. He'll kill you both.'

'Nyssa,' said the Doctor sharply. 'Go and wait in the TARDIS – please.'

With a last anguished look at the Doctor, Nyssa ran out of the room.

The Doctor turned back to Borusa. 'Even if I discover where Omega is hiding, will the TARDIS be able to leave now that Omega controls the Matrix?'

'We will contrive a way for you to leave, Doctor. We must.'

The Doctor nodded accepting the inevitable. 'Then with your permission, Lord President, I had better put on the Matrix Crown.

The Doctor sat in the council chamber in Borusa's chair, the Matrix Crown on his head, his face reflecting enormous strain. Only his body was present.

His mind was in the Matrix.

As soon as the Doctor appeared in the Matrix, Omega materialised to confront him. 'Well, Doctor?'

'It seems you have won, Omega. We can't stop you now.'

'It is unfortunate that it took the death of Hedin to convince you of that.'

'It was an accident. He died for your sake – saving me.'

'Why are you here?'

'I am concerned for Tegan. Is she still safe?'

'She is.'

'Then prove it. Let me speak to her.'

'Very well.'

The figure of Tegan appeared. 'Help us, Doctor. We're in an underground crypt, behind a fountain.'

'Silence, girl,' thundered Omega.

Tegan's form twisted beneath his anger.

The Doctor said, 'You've won Omega. Even if I knew where you were I can't leave Gallifrey, not with you in control of the Matrix.' Suddenly the Doctor snapped, 'Tegan *where are you?*'

'Holland,' gasped Tegan. 'Amsterdam.'

'Be silent, girl, or you will die,' warned Omega.

'J.H.C.' shouted Tegan. Her image distorted and she vanished.

'Omega, is she unharmed?' asked the Doctor urgently.

'Of course, Doctor. She will remain so – as long as you do not work against me.'

Omega's image faded. The Doctor was alone.

In the council chamber, the Matrix Crown rose above the Doctor's head, and he opened his eyes.

'Did you discover Omega's location, Doctor?' asked Borusa eagerly.

'Well, I've narrowed it down to one city – Amsterdam.'

'But the precise location?'

'Not yet. At least I have a clue. The question now is – how do I get away from Gallifrey?'

In the computer room, Damon looked round the circle of distinguished visitors, feeling somewhat over-whelmed. 'How can I serve you, Lord President?'

'The Doctor's TARDIS must leave Gallifrey

undetected. Is there any way we can distract Omega meanwhile?'

Damon shook his head. 'I doubt it. I've already tested all the by-pass circuits. Omega has cut us off.'

Suddenly Thalia said, 'What about a pulse-loop?'

Borusa smiled. 'Of course. Brilliantly simple, Lady Thalia. Install a pulse-loop at once, Damon.'

Damon hurried away.

'And what exactly is a pulse-loop?' demanded Zorac querulously.

'It is a simple device used to trace faults on the Master Circuits.'

'It has a photon pulse, you see,' explained Thalia. 'Omega will have to spend time tracking it down and neutralising it, just to be sure we're not trying to by-pass Master Control.'

'It will create both distraction and confusion,' said Borusa. 'Enough, we hope, to allow the doctor's TARDIS to leave Gallifrey unnoticed.'

Nyssa was waiting anxiously when the Doctor came back into the TARDIS control room. She gave him an accusing look. 'Well?'

'It's all right,' said the Doctor soothingly. 'I contacted Tegan, she's unharmed, and she managed to give me some idea of where Omega is.'

A light flashed on the scanner screen, and the face of Borusa appeared. 'Doctor? I think we've found the distraction we need!'

In the computer room, everything was ready.

Borusa contacted the TARDIS. 'Are you ready to leave, Doctor?' On the screen he could see the Doctor poised at the controls.

'As soon as you give the word.'

'Very well.' Borusa nodded to Damon who slotted a programme cassette into the console and punched in instructions. 'Everything is ready, Lord President.'

'Then activate.'

Damon pressed the control and shouted, 'Now!'

Borusa leaned over the communicator. 'Go, Doctor. Go now!'

The Doctor was working frantically at the controls. Slowly, very slowly, the time-rotor began its rise and fall.

Borusa switched the computer room scanner to an outside view of the TARDIS.

They heard the familiar wheezing, groaning sound and the TARDIS faded away.

'He's gone!' said Borusa.

Damon was checking readings. 'There seems to be a good deal of disturbance in the Matrix, Lord President, just as we planned. Omega must be thoroughly confused.'

Borusa sighed. 'For the Doctor's sake, I hope you're right.'

The Doctor was checking over a small, flat piece of equipment which he had brought from Gallifrey. When the case was clamped back into place it looked like a small metal discus.

Nyssa looked up from the controls. 'We're almost ready to materialise.' She saw what the Doctor was doing. 'What's that thing for, Doctor?'

'It's a fusion breaker. Omega's using a fusion booster to build up the power he needs for a massive energy transfer. If we can find the booster and attach this, it will knock it out of phase.'

'Won't that be dangerous?'

'Only to Omega, I hope. It should feed the power back through his own equipment.'

'A sort of built-in short-circuit?'

'Exactly. Have you got that meter?'

Nyssa held up the meter − a hand-sized black box, with controls and a dial. 'It's calibrated to detect changes in anti-matter.'

A wisp of smoke came from the impulse-loop console. Damon leapt back, just in time as the entire console exploded into flames. 'Omega's discovered the pulse loop − and destroyed it.'

Borusa nodded. It was not to be expected that Omega would be deceived for very long. 'Let us hope that it gave the Doctor the time he needed.'

The time-rotor ceased its rise and fall and all was silent. The Doctor switched on the scanner. He saw a busy city square, people, bicycles, trams, and there in the distance a canal. 'I don't believe it.'

'Believe what?'

'We've actually made it. It's Amsterdam! Come on.'

The Doctor picked up both fusion breaker and anti-matter detector and they hurried from the control room.

Although Colin had emerged from his zombie-like state, it was clear that the experience had weakened him dangerously. Tegan knelt beside him anxiously, wiping his perspiring face with a handkerchief.

It seemed unbearably hot. Through the door to the

control room they could hear the steady roar of some tremendous energy-source.

Robin mopped his forehead with his sleeve. 'Sounds like a power-house in there!'

Tegan nodded, too worried about Colin to pay much attention.

The TARDIS had materialised on the corner of one of Amsterdam's many little squares, and the tolerant citizens paid it remarkably little attention. Maybe they thought it was part of some British tourist drive, like the occasional London double-decker bus.

The Doctor and Nyssa emerged unquestioned. Even their rather unusual style of dress attracted little attention.

Now they were walking through the city centre, too distracted by their quest to register much of the animated scene around them.

'Where are we going, Doctor?' asked Nyssa. 'How do you know where to start looking?'

'When I spoke to Tegan, in the Matrix, she mentioned two things. Her cousin Colin, and the J.H.C.'

'Well?'

'Tegan risked her life to give me that information, so it must mean something. If we can find out what J.H.C. means, it might lead us to Tegan – and to Omega.'

'Where are you going to start?'

'Right here,' said the Doctor. They were outside a telephone box. 'We'll start with the telephone directory.'

'You're dealing with a renegade Time Lord, Doctor. You're not likely to find his address in the phone book!'

The Doctor grinned. 'You never know.' He popped

inside the box, and started leafing through the
directory. 'Now let me see. J.H.C. . . . J.H.C. . . . Here
we are! J.H.C. Jeugdherberg Centrale. Youth hostels!
It must be where they were staying. There aren't all
that many, not in the centre. We can give them a ring.'
The Doctor felt through all his pockets and looked
appealingly at Nyssa. 'I don't suppose you happen to
have any Dutch money?'

Nyssa searched through her pockets and found three
very oddly shaped coins. Clearly they weren't going to
fit into a Dutch telephone box.

The Doctor looked at them. 'Is that it?'

'I'm afraid so.'

The Doctor sighed. He took out the anti-matter
meter and switched it on. It was on a very low reading,
just past zero. 'Anti-matter present but low-level and
steady,' he muttered. 'Omega can't have transferred
yet. But it won't be much longer.'

Nyssa tapped the meter. 'Can't we find him with
this?'

'If only it were that simple. It's non-directional you
see, registers presence but not location.' He put the
meter away.

'What now?'

The Doctor was scribbling down addresses in his
diary. 'No other choice. We'll just have to check every
hostel on foot.'

'Can't we use the TARDIS?'

'And alert Omega?' The Doctor shook his head. 'We
daren't risk it. Come on, the first one's this way.'

In the computer room Damon was staring in horror at
an instrument dial.

'The power build-up is tremendous, Lord President.

Omega's transfer must be imminent!'

In the control room of Omega's TARDIS, the power build-up was almost complete.

Omega sat in his chair, linked to the console, energy vibrating through his body.

Slowly the skin-tight face-mask began to crack and peel away.

11

Transference

The Doctor and Nyssa came wearily down the steps of
their third youth hostel. No Tegan Jovanka, no Colin
Frazer.

Nyssa looked at the Doctor. 'You know, this could
take forever?'

'Well, there's no other way.'

'That last receptionist wasn't very friendly. What if
she was being difficult, choosing not to remember
Tegan?'

'We've just got to carry on, Nyssa,' said the Doctor
wearily.

'Can't the Time Lords help us?'

'Not now. They've done all they can in getting us
here. Now it's up to us.'

The Doctor and Nyssa went on their way, not
realising that since neither Tegan nor Colin had ever
actually stayed in an Amsterdam hostel, the chances of
finding anyone who remembered them were non-
existent.

They were walking along the edge of one of the canals
when the Doctor thought to check the meter again. To
his horror the anti-matter reading was higher – much
higher. 'It looks as if Omega is about to transfer.' The
Doctor thought for a moment. 'We'll try one more place

together, Nyssa, then we must split up. It'll double our chances.'

'How long have we got?'

The Doctor looked at the needle on the meter, now very close to the danger zone. 'I don't know. But it can't be long.'

By now the power-throb from the control room was shaking the whole ante-room.

Tegan, Colin and Robin huddled together, terrified by the forces that seemed about to overwhelm them.

The young man on duty at the reception desk was polite, patient and helpful. But the answer to the Doctor's urgent question was the same. 'I am sorry. We have no record of a Miss Tegan Jovanka.'

'What about her cousin?'

'Do you have the name, sir?'

'Colin, I think. I don't know the surname.'

'In that case, sir . . .' The receptionist spread his hands helplessly.

'Yes, of course. I'm sorry.' The Doctor managed a smile. 'Well, thanks anyway. Come on Nyssa.'

They were heading for the door when the receptionist called after them, 'Excuse me, did you say your friend was from Australia?'

The Doctor turned back. 'Yes, that's right. Why?'

The receptionist was checking through the register. 'I don't know if it's of any help. There *was* an Australian booked in, a Colin Frazer. He failed to arrive it seems, but I believe his friend turned up. I was not on duty myself. One moment please.' He disappeared into the little inner office.

Nyssa was beginning to despair. 'Isn't there

something else we could do, Doctor?'

'No. Tegan is our only link.'

The receptionist returned with a tall blond girl with her hair in a pony-tail. 'Excuse me, you were asking about a Miss Jovanka?'

'We were indeed,' said the Doctor hopefully.

The girl looked troubled. 'Mr Stuart . . . the friend of the Australian Mr Frazer who did not arrive – left a note for a Miss Jovanka. Then he himself failed to return. He said I was to give this to her if he missed her at the airport and she came on here.' She produced a sealed envelope from under the counter.

The Doctor held out his hand. 'May I see the note?'

'I am not sure if I should . . .'

'Please,' said Nyssa urgently. 'It's terribly important that we find her, and this may be our only chance.'

The girl shrugged and handed over the envelope.

Eagerly the Doctor ripped it open and read the note. It was from Robin to Tegan, written the morning before he set off to meet her at the airport, telling her that Colin had disappeared when they were staying at a place called Frankendael. The note warned her not to go there herself, but to try the police.

The Doctor looked up. 'Do you know a house called Frankendael?'

'Yes. It is not far from here.'

Looking round, the Doctor saw a wall-map. 'Can you show me please? It's very urgent.'

'Of course.' The receptionist came over to the map. 'It is not far away – just here.' She pointed.

'Thanks!' Grabbing Nyssa's hand, the Doctor ran from the hostel. They sprinted down the street, almost bowling over a shopping-laden Dutch housewife in their haste.

To Nyssa's irritation, the Doctor stopped to help pick up her shopping before hurrying on.

They hurried down the canal-side, over one bridge and then another, down a quiet tree-lined street, and finally arrived at a handsome old house set back from the road.

'This must be it,' said the Doctor. 'Frankendael.'

Nyssa surveyed the house. 'Can't see any sign of a crypt. Maybe it's round the back somewhere.'

The Doctor took out the anti-matter meter. The needle was at maximum, quivering furiously. 'It's a matter of minutes now.' He spotted a gleam of water through the trees. 'The fountain! Tegan said it was behind the fountain!'

Slipping the meter in his pocket he ran towards the house, Nyssa close behind him.

It didn't take them long to find the flight of steps. They reached the bottom, opened the door to the crypt and went cautiously inside, daylight flooding through the doorway behind them.

They looked round, seeing only what you would expect to see in a crypt – a variety of tombs in different shapes and sizes.

'Where could they be?' whispered Nyssa.

'Depends what shape Omega has given his TARDIS. Listen!'

A steady roar of power was coming from the far side of the crypt.

They walked through the crypt to the pump house and went inside. The Doctor looked at the network of pipes around the walls. 'A pumping system. Perfect. Just perfect for Omega.'

'Why, Doctor?'

'Omega must have located the curve of the Arc in

Amsterdam, below sea-level to maintain pressure for conversion.'

He spotted the horseshoe-shaped device clamped to the machinery. 'And here's the fusion booster from Gallifrey.' Highly delighted, the Doctor took the fusion breaker from his pocket, adjusted the setting and began attaching it to the fusion booster.

The Doctor was completely absorbed in his work, and Nyssa was watching him. Both had their backs to the door that led to the crypt.

Neither of them noticed when the door to Omega's TARDIS slid open and the insectoid Ergon emerged, a weapon in its hands. It began moving towards the pump house.

The Doctor finished attaching the fusion breaker and pressed a control. The device began humming with power.

Nyssa heard movement behind her and spun round.

The Ergon stood in the doorway, weapon raised, about to fire. Nyssa screamed and shoved the Doctor clear.

The energy blast from the Ergon's weapon struck the wall. A large chunk of masonry flashed positive and negative and simply disappeared.

The Doctor sprang at the Ergon, grappling with it before it could fire again. Taking the thing by surprise, the Doctor managed to wrench the weapon from the creature's hands. It clattered to the floor.

Seizing the Doctor's neck in its stubby claws, the Ergon made a determined attempt to throttle him. The Doctor fought back as best he could, but the lizard-like creature was appallingly strong.

Nyssa snatched up the weapon, but the Doctor and the Ergon were so close together, she dared not fire.

With a last despairing effort, the Doctor swung the Ergon round, giving Nyssa a clear shot at its back.

'Nyssa,' croaked the Doctor. 'Fire! Fire!'

Nyssa fired, and the monster staggered back, crashing to the floor.

In his TARDIS Omega twisted convulsively and shrieked as his link with the Ergon was brutally severed.

The Doctor looked down at the shrivelled creature, rubbing the bruises its claws had left in his neck.

'What was it?' gasped Nyssa.

'An Ergon. One of Omega's less successful atempts at psycho-synthesis. Quickly, Nyssa.'

Taking the Ergon's weapon from Nyssa's hands, the Doctor led the way to the open door of Omega's TARDIS.

They ran into the control room, which by now was filled with a shattering roar of power. Smoke filled the air and the whole console seemed to glow with heat.

The most incredible sight of all was Omega himself. The stylised mask had degenerated into a horrific twisted mess, with areas of underskin visible through the parts that had peeled away. It was like seeing a snake that had only partly succeeded in sloughing off its old skin.

Omega said, 'Drop the weapon, Doctor. I have taken precautions. Drop the weapon or the Earth girl dies.'

Omega gestured, and Tegan appeared behind him, trapped in a light beam that was clearly some kind of force-field.

The Doctor threw down the Ergon's weapon. 'It's too

late, Omega. You can't transfer now.'

'You are wrong, Doctor. By now I have all the energy I need.'

Suddenly a great white-hot beam of light arced across the control room.

'What have you done?' shrieked Omega. 'What have you done?'

In the pump house the fusion breaker was emitting a high-pitched hum of energy as it took the fusion booster into overload. Suddenly the booster glowed white-hot and exploded.

The Doctor raised his voice above the din. 'The Arc of Infinity is shifting! Go now, Omega. Return to your own universe while you still have the chance.'

Omega was too obsessed to listen. 'I must transfer. I must cease to be anti-matter and live again.'

A peeling hand reached out for the transfer switch.

'Down, Nyssa,' shouted the Doctor.

He threw himself to the floor, dragging Nyssa with him. The force-field holding Tegan cut out, and she collapsed.

Omega's console, and the very chair in which he sat, began glowing with incandescent heat. Omega threw himself from the chair, as the console exploded.

12

Omega's Freedom

The control room was a shambles, a smoking pile of wrecked equipment. Painfully, the Doctor picked himself up. He saw Nyssa lying nearby, and helped her to rise.

On the other side of the control room, Tegan too was struggling to her feet.

Then from the wreckage that had once been his control console Omega arose. The material that formed the once skin-tight mask was hanging in charred strips so that he looked like the victim of some terrible accident. 'Yes, Doctor. I live!'

'You have failed, Omega. The bond is not complete.'

Omega laughed. 'Is it not, Doctor? Watch!'

The Doctor and his companions watched Omega raise trembling fingers and begin peeling the remains of the mask from his face. As the fragments of mask came away, a face was revealed beneath them. It was one that the Doctor knew well. The face was his own. Omega had transformed himself into a replica of the Doctor. Temporarily at least, the bonding was complete.

'You see, Doctor?' said Omega exultantly. 'You see?' His voice was low and harsh, quite unlike the Doctor's, but face and body were identical.

'It's not permanent,' cried the Doctor desperately. 'It

will fail, Omega, revert to anti-matter.'

'You are wrong Doctor. I have life again.' Omega looked around at the wreckage of the control room. 'You have destroyed my TARDIS, but it is of no importance. I shall build another. Expect me on Gallifrey – soon.'

Omega strode from the control room.

Nyssa said, 'Quickly, Doctor, we've got to get after him.'

The Doctor was rummaging in the wreckage. 'I must find the matter-converter, the Ergon's weapon. I can't destroy Omega without it. Nyssa, Tegan, help me.'

Tegan shook her head. 'I've got to find Colin and Robin.'

She disappeared through the inner door. Nyssa and the Doctor began rooting through the debris of the control room.

Omega stood in the garden outside the big house, looking at the grass and the trees and the flowers. He threw back his head and gave a great laugh. To be alive again, in a real world! A world that, like all worlds, would soon be under his control.

Omega decided to go out and survey his kingdom. He looked at his tattered cloak. First he would need suitable clothing. Some little way away an overalled gardener was tending a flower-bed. Omega moved towards him.

The Doctor straightened up with a sigh of relief, the matter-converter in his hands.

Tegan ran back into the control room. 'Colin seems a lot better. Robin's going to get him to a hospital.'

'Good, good,' said the Doctor. 'Now hurry! We've

got to find Omega, before it's too late.'

In the computer room, Borusa and the High Council were gathered anxiously around Damon, who was studying the readings on a console.

Damon looked up his face worried. 'It seems the Doctor has failed. There is anti-matter present in our Universe. It's shielded, but it's building up fast.'

The Doctor, Nyssa and Tegan were standing over the dead body of the gardener. The body was sprawled at the edge of a flower-bed, with Omega's cloak cast carelessly over it.

'Did Omega kill him?' asked Tegan.

'Yes. No doubt he wanted to hide himself in the crowd.'

'What happens if we don't find him?'

'The biggest explosion this part of the Universe is ever likely to witness,' said the Doctor simply. 'Come on.'

They headed for the street.

There was an organ in the street not far from the house, a huge ornately decorated affair. Predictably enough, it was playing 'Tulips from Amsterdam'.

Street organs are a common enough sight in Amsterdam, but nothing was common or usual to Omega. Eyes filled with wonder, like a new-born child, he walked towards the organ. A handful of adults and children were gathered round it and Omega joined them.

Someone jostled past him. Omega looked down angrily to see a small boy wriggling his way to the front.

The boy turned and gave him a cheeky grin. Just for a

second, Omega glared down at him, and then his lips twitched in a reluctant smile. The boy turned back to the organ, completely absorbed, and Omega watched too with the same child-like fascination.

The Doctor looked up and down the street and heard the strains of the organ.

Omega tired of the organ after a while and moved on. He stood on one of the old bridges, staring down at the canal. Then he caught sight of his own hands, resting on the parapet. The skin was beginning to blacken and peel.

The Doctor, Nyssa and Tegan moved on past the organ. The Doctor studied the anti-matter meter.

'He can't be far ahead.'

'How much time do we have?' asked Nyssa.

'I don't know. Omega's magnetic shielding is in accelerated decay by now.'

'What'll happen when it goes,' asked Tegan.

'He'll revert to anti-matter. Anti-matter — in our Universe.'

Omega hurried on his way — and became aware that passers-by were reacting to him with horror and disgust. He put his hand to his face — he could feel it erupting into decaying lumps. The Doctor had been right. His new body was unstable . . .

At the edge of a canal the Doctor and his two companions halted, breathless. There was no sign of Omega.

'It's no good,' said the Doctor wearily. 'We've lost him.'

There was a bridge further along the canal and

beside it a little knot of people.

Tegan pointed. 'Look, Doctor. There's something happening up there.'

They ran towards the bridge and found a sobbing, hysterical flower-seller, surrounded by passers-by trying to calm her down, and presumably asking her what was the matter, what had frightened her. The flower-seller pointed.

The Doctor looked and saw a shambling overalled figure hurrying across the bridge. 'It's Omega!' shouted the Doctor. 'Come on!'

Damon looked up from the console. 'It's still building up. Can't be much longer now.'

Zorac said agitatedly. 'Even if the Doctor finds the source he'll never be able to contain it.'

By now the Castellan had come to join them. 'I have learned that it is unwise to predict what the Doctor can and cannot do.'

The Doctor and his companions pursued Omega over the bridge along the side of the canal – and found that he was nowhere in sight.

'We've lost him,' said Tegan.

The Doctor stared along the length of the canal. 'I see you Omega,' he called, quite untruthfully.

The bluff worked. Suddenly Omega ducked out of his hiding-place behind an oil drum, and started running.

The Doctor and the two girls ran after him.

Omega turned away from the canal and ran across the main street. He moved in a strange lurching run, as if his body wasn't working properly.

The Doctor and the others tried to follow, but the way was blocked by one of Amsterdam's huge yellow trams. By the time it had passed, Omega had disappeared again.

As they hesitated, uncertain which way to go, they heard a clattering of metal and a yell of anger and pain. 'This way,' shouted the Doctor.

They ran towards the sound. It came from a narrow alleyway between two tall buildings. In the middle of the alleyway, a man in a chef's hat was lying sprawled amidst some overturned dustbins.

The Doctor helped him up.

'Are you okay?' asked Tegan. 'What happened?'

The man answered with a stream of what sounded very much like Dutch curses, and pointed angrily down the alley. Presumably Omega had knocked him down in his headlong flight.

'He'll be all right,' said the Doctor. 'Come on!'

They emerged from the alleyway – just in time to see Omega cross an open square and disappear down yet another street.

They followed.

When they reached the top of the street, Omega had disappeared again.

Some of the houses in the street had outside staircases leading up to the front doors. Omega was crouched motionless in the dark space beneath one of these stairways. He stayed quite still, as the Doctor and his companions walked past his hiding-place.

The Doctor stared down the street. It was long and straight, and seemed empty for a very long way ahead. Surely Omega should be in sight by now.

Tegan shook her head. 'He's got away.'

'He can't have,' said Nyssa despairingly.

They heard a frantic barking and growling from

somewhere close behind them and turned round.

An old gentleman was walking his dog along the street. The dog was snarling ferociously at the dark space under one of the stairways.

As they watched, an overalled figure with a horribly disfigured face sprang out from beneath the stairs and ran back down the street towards the canal.

The Doctor and his friends ran in pursuit.

They chased Omega back up the street, across the main road and along the canal bank towards another bridge. But Omega had chosen the wrong bridge this time.

Just before he reached it, it rose slowly in the air to admit the passage of a boat too big to go underneath.

Angrily Omega turned back towards the nearby lock. He ran blindly along a short stone jetty and stopped at the end. He turned and saw the Doctor and the two Earth girls coming towards him. Omega was trapped.

When the Doctor and his companions reached the end of the jetty, Omega was slumped despairingly against a bollard. He looked up at them, and the two girls recoiled in horror.

Omega was a terrifying sight. His face and hands, and presumably the body beneath the overalls, were literally decaying. The face was twisted and malformed, the features already beginning to liquefy.

The Doctor looked sadly down at him. 'I warned you this would happen, Omega.'

Omega's voice was slurred. 'Things could have been . . . different . . . Doctor. The power and greatness of Omega . . . could have been yours. But no . . . your hatred of . . .'

'I didn't hate you, Omega. None of us hated you. Why couldn't you be content to survive as you were?'

'It was time to come home, Doctor,' croaked the misshapen figure. 'Time to find peace . . . to rest.' With sudden anger, Omega struggled to get up. 'It is over now, Doctor,' he snarled. 'Now all must die.'

The Doctor produced the matter-converter from beneath his coat.

The malformed lips twisted in a ghastly smile. 'You'll never have the courage to use it, Doctor.'

'I can expel or destroy you, Omega. The choice is yours.'

'It is too late, Doctor. What you offer is worse than death. If I am to be denied life, then all things must perish. All things!' Omega fell back writhing.

'What's he trying to do, Doctor?' whispered Tegan.

'He's willing his own destruction, accelerating the shielding decay.' The Doctor raised his voice. 'Don't force me, Omega.'

'Farewell, Doctor,' croaked Omega. Smoke began rising from his body.

'Stop him!' screamed Tegan.

The Doctor hesitated. But there was really no alternative. In seconds now, Omega's body would revert to anti-matter and the resulting explosion would be catastrophic.

The Doctor fired. A beam of light shot from the weapon, and Omega's body jerked and twisted. He gave a terrible scream and a chain-reaction of explosions ran through his body. As the smoke cleared, Omega faded and disappeared. The Doctor lowered the matter-converter. 'It's over,' he said quietly and turned away.

In the computer room, President Borusa, Thalia, Cardinal Zorac and the Castellan watched tensely as

116

Damon checked readings on his console.

When he looked up, Damon was smiling. 'The Doctor did it – somehow. The anti-matter source is gone. Omega must have been destroyed.'

For once Lord President Borusa was looking his years. 'Unfortunate, wretched creature. My only hope is that he has found peace at last.'

The Doctor and Nyssa stood outside a telephone box in Amsterdam's central railway station, waiting for Tegan to finish her call.

'Doctor, is Omega really dead?' asked Nyssa suddenly.

The Doctor said enigmatically. 'He seemed to die before, yet he returned to confound us all.'

Tegan came out of the box. 'Well, I'm sure you'll be pleased to hear Colin will be out of hospital soon, and on his way back to Brisbane. Robin's going home too – they've even given him a new passport.'

'Excellent!' said the Doctor cheerfully.

'What about you, Tegan?' asked Nyssa.

'Me, I'm indestructible. Really, I'm fine.'

The Doctor beamed at her. 'Well, it's been marvellous seeing you again.'

'Yes, indeed,' said Nyssa warmly. 'I've missed you, you know. I do wish you didn't have to go back to your job.'

'What job?' said Tegan cheerfully. 'Didn't I tell you? I got the sack.'

Nyssa hugged her delightedly. 'Wonderful.'

Tegan looked challengingly at the Doctor. 'So – you're stuck with me, aren't you?'

The Doctor smiled wryly. 'So it seems.'

Curiously enough, he found he didn't mind at all.

DOCTOR WHO

0426114558	TERRANCE DICKS **Doctor Who and The** **Abominable Snowmen**	**£1.35**
0426200373	**Doctor Who and The** **Android Invasion**	**£1.25**
0426201086	**Doctor Who and The** **Androids of Tara**	**£1.25**
0426116313	IAN MARTER **Doctor Who and The** **Ark in Space**	**£1.25**
0426201043	TERRANCE DICKS **Doctor Who and The** **Armageddon Factor**	**£1.25**
0426112954	**Doctor Who and The** **Auton Invasion**	**£1.50**
0426116747	**Doctor Who and The** **Brain of Morbius**	**£1.35**
0426110250	**Doctor Who and The** **Carnival of Monsters**	**£1.25**
042611471X	MALCOLM HULKE **Doctor Who and** **The Cave Monsters**	**£1.50**
0426117034	TERRANCE DICKS **Doctor Who and The** **Claws of Axos**	**£1.35**
042620123X	DAVID FISHER **Doctor Who and The** **Creature from the Pit**	**£1.25**
0426113160	DAVID WHITAKER **Doctor Who and The Crusaders**	**£1.50**
0426200616	BRIAN HAYLES **Doctor Who and The Curse** **of Peladon**	**£1.50**
0426114639	GERRY DAVIS **Doctor Who and The Cybermen**	**£1.50**
0426113322	BARRY LETTS **Doctor Who and The Daemons**	**£1.50**

Prices are subject to alteration

DOCTOR WHO

0426101103	DAVID WHITAKER **Doctor Who and The** **Daleks**	£1.50
042611244X	TERRANCE DICKS **Doctor Who and The Dalek** **Invasion of Earth**	£1.25
0426103807	**Doctor Who and The Day** **of the Daleks**	£1.35
042620042X	**Doctor Who – Death to** **the Daleks**	£1.35
0426119657	**Doctor Who and The** **Deadly Assassin**	£1.25
0426200969	**Doctor Who and The** **Destiny of the Daleks**	£1.35
0426108744	MALCOLM HULKE **Doctor Who and The** **Dinosaur Invasion**	£1.35
0426103726	**Doctor Who and** **The Doomsday Weapon**	£1.35
0426201464	IAN MARTER **Doctor Who and The** **Enemy of the World**	£1.25
0426200063	TERRANCE DICKS **Doctor Who and The** **Face of Evil**	£1.25
0426201507	ANDREW SMITH **Doctor Who – Full Circle**	£1.35
0426112601	TERRANCE DICKS **Doctor Who and The** **Genesis of the Daleks**	£1.35
0426112792	**Doctor Who and The Giant Robot**	£1.25
0426115430	MALCOLM HULKE **Doctor Who and The** **Green Death**	£1.35

rices are subject to alteration

STAR Books are obtainable from many booksellers and newsagents. If you have any difficulty please send purchase price plus postage on the scale below to:-

Star Cash Sales
P.O. Box 11
Falmouth
Cornwall
OR
Star Book Service,
G.P.O. Box 29,
Douglas,
Isle of Man,
British Isles.

While every effort is made to keep prices low, it is sometimes necessary to increase prices at short notice. Star Books reserve the right to show new retail prices on covers which may differ from those advertised in the text or elsewhere.

Postage and Packing Rate
UK: 45p for the first book, 20p for the second book and 14p for each additional book ordered to a maximum charge of £1.63. BFPO and EIRE: 45p for the first book, 20p for the second book, 14p per copy for the next 7 books thereafter 8p per book. Overseas: 75p for the first book and 21p per copy for each additional book.